Contemporary
Stories 2

Selected and edited by
Nick Jones

Oxford University Press   1989

Oxford University Press, Walton Street, Oxford OX2 6DP

Oxford New York Toronto
Delhi Bombay Calcutta Madras Karachi
Petaling Jaya Singapore Hong Kong Tokyo
Nairobi Dar es Salaam Cape Town
Melbourne Auckland

and associated companies in
 Berlin Ibadan

Oxford is a trade mark of Oxford University Press

ISBN 019 831254 7

Set by Pentacor Ltd, High Wycombe, Bucks
Printed in Great Britain at the University Press, Cambridge

Contents

Acknowledgements

The Editor and publishers are grateful for permission to include the following copyright material:

Ama Ata Aidoo: 'In the Cutting of a Drink' from **No Sweetness Here** (Longman African Classic, new ed. 1988. First publ. 1970). Reprinted by permission of Longman Group (UK) Ltd.

Margaret Atwood: 'Significant Moments in the Life of My Mother' from **Bluebeard's Egg & Other Stories**. (Jonathan Cape Ltd, 1988). ******

Murray Bail: 'The Drover's Wife' from **The Drover's Wife and Other Stories** (1986). Reprinted by permission of Faber & Faber Ltd.

Russell Banks: 'Queen for a Day' from **Success Stories**. (1986). Reprinted by permission of Hamish Hamilton Ltd.

Neil Bissoondath: 'In the Kingdom of the Golden Dust' from **Digging Up the Mountains** (1986). Reprinted by permission of Andre Deutsch Ltd.

Angela Carter: 'The Werewolf' from **The Bloody Chamber and Other Stories** (1979). Reprinted by permission of Victor Gollancz Ltd.

Robert Carter: 'Kid in a Bin' from **The Pleasure Within** (1987). Reprinted by permission of Angus & Robertson (UK).

Peter Cary: 'Do You Love Me?' from **The Fat Man in History**. Reprinted by permission of Faber & Faber Ltd.

Mary Flanagan: 'White Places' from **Bad Girls** (1984). Reprinted by permission of Jonathan Cape Ltd.

Ellen Gilchrist: 'Revenge' from **In The Land of Dreamy Dreams** (1981). Reprinted by permission of Faber & Faber Ltd.

Christopher Hope: 'Learning to Fly' from **Private Parts**. Reprinted by permission of A. P. Watt Ltd., on behalf of the author.

Keri Hulme: 'Tally of the Souls of Sheep' from **The Windeater/Te Kaihau**. Copyright 1986 by Keri Hulme. Reprinted by permission of Hodder & Stoughton Ltd. & Victoria University Press.

Neil Jordan: 'Tree' from **Night in Tunisia**. (1983). Reprinted by permission of Neil Jordan and Anthony Sheil Associates Ltd.

James Kelman: 'No Longer the Warehouseman' from **Not Not While the Giro** (Polygon Books). Reprinted with permission.

Jamaica Kincaid: 'Girl' is taken from **At The Bottom of The River** (Picador 1984). Reprinted by permission of Pan Books Ltd.

Bernard Mac Laverty: 'Father and Son' from **A Time to Dance**. Reprinted by permission of Jonathan Cape Ltd.

Michelene Wandor: 'Sweet Sixteen' from **Guests in the Body**. (1986). Reprinted by permission of Virago Press.

Preface

This collection has been prompted by the success of **Contemporary Stories** (OUP 1986), and has been compiled on similar principles. Most of the stories have been published in the last few years, the earliest in 1970. As in the previous collection, there is a conscious diversity of cultural origin, and a variety of perspectives on the world. In selecting the stories, I have paid particular attention to the richness and diversity of narrative forms and voices, to the many different ways in which a story can be told. The collection can be expected to appeal strongly to a wide range of readers in the 14–18 age group, and is appropriate for literary study at that level.

There is a Commentary at the end of the book for those who might find it useful, including pointers to further reading. The Ideas for Discussion are not intended to be addressed systematically, as an agenda of questions to be answered, but rather as an attempt to share one reader's experience of the process of reading and understanding the stories, and to prompt further responses. The Ideas for Writing are offered as brief starting-points for explorations of the stories through written assignments; students and teachers alike will no doubt wish to adapt and expand them to suit their own ideas and approaches.

The Commentary assumes a context in which stories are read both silently and to others, reflected upon, and talked over; and in which the re-reading, re-telling, and re-working of stories is a natural extension of the reading process. The assumption, in other words, is that imaginative, imitative and re-creative responses to literary texts are at least as valuable as discursive criticism, and as capable both of deepening and of demonstrating a reader's critical understanding.

Nick Jones

Revenge

Ellen Gilchrist

It was the summer of the Broad Jump Pit.

The Broad Jump Pit, how shall I describe it! It was a bright orange rectangle in the middle of a green pasture. It was three feet deep, filled with river sand and sawdust. A real cinder track led up to it, ending where tall poles for pole-vaulting rose forever in the still Delta air.

I am looking through the old binoculars. I am watching Bunky coming at a run down the cinder path, pausing expertly at the Jump-off line, then rising into the air, heels stretched far out in front of him, landing in the sawdust. Before the dust has settled Saint John comes running with the tape, calling out measurements in his high, excitable voice.

Next comes my thirteen-year-old brother, Dudley, coming at a brisk jog down the track, the pole-vaulting pole held lightly in his delicate hands, then vaulting, high into the sky. His skinny tanned legs make a last, desperate surge, and he is clear and over.

Think how it looked from my lonely exile atop the chicken house. I was ten years old, the only girl in a house full of cousins. There were six of us, shipped to the Delta for the summer, dumped on my grandmother right in the middle of a world war.

They built this wonder in answer to a V-Mail letter from my father in Europe. The war was going well, my father wrote, within a year the Allies would triumph over the forces of evil, the world would be at peace, and the Olympic torch would again be brought down from its mountain and carried to Zurich or Amsterdam or London or Mexico City, wherever free men lived and worshipped sports. My father had been a participant in an Olympic event when he was young.

Therefore, the letter continued, Dudley and Bunky and Philip

1

and Saint John and Oliver were to begin training. The United States would need athletes now, not soldiers.

They were to train for broad jumping and pole-vaulting and discus throwing, for fifty-, one-hundred-, and four-hundred-yard dashes, for high and low hurdles. The letter included instructions for building the pit, for making pole-vaulting poles out of cane, and for converting ordinary sawhorses into hurdles. It ended with a page of tips for proper eating and admonished Dudley to take good care of me as I was my father's own dear sweet little girl.

The letter came one afternoon. Early the next morning they began construction. Around noon I wandered out to the pasture to see how they were coming along. I picked up a shovel.

'Put that down, Rhoda,' Dudley said. 'Don't bother us now. We're working.'

'I know it,' I said. 'I'm going to help.'

'No, you're not,' Bunky said. 'This is the Broad Jump Pit. We're starting our training.'

'I'm going to do it too,' I said. 'I'm going to be in training.'

'Get out of here now,' Dudley said. 'This is only for boys, Rhoda. This isn't a game.'

'I'm going to dig it if I want to,' I said, picking up a shovelful of dirt and throwing it on Philip. On second thought I picked up another shovelful and threw it on Bunky.

'Get out of here, Ratface,' Philip yelled at me. 'You German spy.' He was referring to the initials on my Girl Scout uniform.

'You goddamn niggers.' I yelled. 'You niggers, I'm digging this if I want to and you can't stop me, you nasty niggers, you Japs, you Jews.' I was throwing dirt on everyone now. Dudley grabbed the shovel and wrestled me to the ground. He held my arms down in the coarse grass and peered into my face.

'Rhoda, you're not having anything to do with this Broad Jump Pit. And if you set foot inside this pasture or come around here and touch anything we will break your legs and drown you in the bayou with a crowbar around your neck.' He was twisting my leg until it creaked at the joints. 'Do you get it, Rhoda? Do you understand me?'

'Let me up,' I was screaming, my rage threatening to split open my skull. 'Let me up, you goddamn nigger, you Jap, you spy. I'm telling Grannie and you're going to get the worst whipping of your life. And you better quit digging this hole for the horses to fall in. Let me up, let me up. Let me go.'

'You've been ruining everything we've thought up all summer,' Dudley said, 'and you're not setting foot inside this pasture.'

In the end they dragged me back to the house, and I ran screaming into the kitchen where Grannie and Calvin, the black man who did the cooking, tried to comfort me, feeding me pound cake and offering to let me help with the mayonnaise.

'You be a sweet girl, Rhoda,' my grandmother said, 'and this afternoon we'll go over to Esenglas Plantation to play with Miss Ann Wentzel.'

'I don't want to play with Miss Ann Wentzel,' I screamed. 'I hate Miss Ann Wentzel. She's fat and she calls me a Yankee. She said my socks were ugly.'

'Why, Rhoda,' my grandmother said. 'I'm surprised at you. Miss Ann Wentzel is your own sweet friend. Her momma was your momma's roommate at All Saint's. How can you talk like that?'

'She's a nigger,' I screamed. 'She's a goddamned nigger German spy.'

'Now it's coming. Here comes the temper,' Calvin said, rolling his eyes back in their sockets to make me madder. I threw my second fit of the morning, beating my fists into a door frame. My grandmother seized me in soft arms. She led me to a bedroom where I sobbed myself to sleep in a sea of down pillows.

The construction went on for several weeks. As soon as they finished breakfast every morning they started out for the pasture. Wood had to be burned to make cinders, sawdust brought from the sawmill, sand hauled up from the riverbank by wheelbarrow.

When the pit was finished the savage training began. From my several vantage points I watched them. Up and down, up and down they ran, dove, flew, sprinted. Drenched with sweat they wrestled each other to the ground in bitter feuds over distances and times and fractions of inches.

Dudley was their self-appointed leader. He drove them like a demon. They began each morning by running around the edge of the pasture several times, then practising their hurdles and dashes, then on to discus throwing and calisthenics. Then on to the Broad Jump Pit with its endless challenges.

They even pressed the old mare into service. Saint John was from New Orleans and knew the British ambassador and was thinking of being a polo player. Up and down the pasture he drove the poor old creature, leaning far out of the saddle, swatting a basketball with my grandaddy's cane.

I spied on them from the swing that went out over the bayou, and from the roof of the chicken house, and sometimes from the pasture fence itself, calling out insults or attempts to make them jealous.

'Guess what,' I would yell, 'I'm going to town to the Chinaman's store.' 'Guess what, I'm getting to go to the beauty parlor.' 'Doctor Biggs says you're adopted.'

They ignored me. At meals they sat together at one end of the table, making jokes about my temper and my red hair, opening their mouths so I could see their half-chewed food, burping loudly in my direction.

At night they pulled their cots together on the sleeping porch, plotting against me while I slept beneath my grandmother's window, listening to the soft assurance of her snoring.

I began to pray the Japs would win the war, would come marching into Issaquena County and take them prisoners, starving and torturing them, sticking bamboo splinters under their fingernails. I saw myself in the Japanese colonel's office, turning them in, writing their names down, myself being treated like an honoured guest, drinking tea from tiny blue cups like the ones the Chinaman had in his store.

They would be outside, tied up with wire. There would be Dudley, begging for mercy. What good to him now his loyal gang, his photographic memory, his trick magnet dogs, his perfect pitch, his camp shorts, his Baby Brownie camera.

I prayed they would get polio, would be consigned forever to iron lungs. I put myself to sleep at night imagining their labored breathing, their five little wheelchairs lined up by the store as I drove by in my father's Packard, my arm around the jacket of his blue uniform, on my way to Hollywood for my screen test.

Meanwhile, I practised dancing. My grandmother had a black housekeeper named Baby Doll who was a wonderful dancer. In the mornings I followed her around while she dusted, begging for dancing lessons. She was a big woman, as tall as a man, and gave off a dark rich smell, an unforgettable incense, a combination of Evening in Paris and the sweet perfume of the cabins.

Baby Doll wore bright skirts and on her blouses a pin that said REMEMBER, then a real pearl, then HARBOR. She was engaged to a sailor and was going to California to be rich as soon as the war was over.

I would put a stack of heavy, scratched records on the record player, and Baby Doll and I would dance through the parlors to the music of Glenn Miller or Guy Lombardo or Tommy Dorsey.

Sometimes I stood on a stool in front of the fireplace and made up lyrics while Baby Doll acted them out, moving lightly across the old dark rugs, turning and swooping and shaking and gliding.

Outside the summer sun beat down on the Delta, beating down a million volts a minute, feeding the soybeans and cotton and clover, sucking Steele's Bayou up into the clouds, beating down on the road and the store, on the pecans and elms and magnolias, on the men at work in the fields, on the athletes at work in the pasture.

Inside Baby Doll and I would be dancing. Or Guy Lombardo would be playing 'Begin the Beguine' and I would be belting out lyrics.

> *'Oh, let them begin . . . we don't care,*
> *America all . . . ways does its share,*
> *We'll be there with plenty of ammo,*
> *Allies . . . don't ever despair . . . '*

Baby Doll thought I was a genius. If I was having an especially creative morning she would go running out to the kitchen and bring anyone she could find to hear me.

'Oh, let them begin any warrr . . . ' I would be singing, tapping one foot against the fireplace tiles, waving my arms around like a conductor.

> *'Uncle Sam will fight*
> *for the underr . . . doggg.*
> *Never fear, Allies, never fear.'*

A new record would drop. Baby Doll would swoop me into her fragrant arms, and we would break into an improvization on Tommy Dorsey's 'Boogie-Woogie.'

But the Broad Jump Pit would not go away. It loomed in my dreams. If I walked to the store I had to pass the pasture. If I stood on the porch or looked out my grandmother's window, there it was, shimmering in the sunlight, constantly guarded by one of the Olympians.

Things went from bad to worse between me and Dudley. If we so much as passed each other in the hall a fight began. He would hold up his fists and dance around, trying to look like a fighter. When I came flailing at him he would reach underneath my arms and punch me in the stomach.

I considered poisoning him. There was a box of while powder in the toolshed with a skull and cross bones above the label. Several times I took it down and held it in my hands, shuddering at the power it gave me. Only the thought of the electric chair kept me from using it.

Every day Dudley gathered his troops and headed out for the pasture. Every day my hatred grew and festered. Then, just about the time I could stand it no longer, a diversion occurred.

One afternoon about four o'clock an official-looking sedan clattered across the bridge and came roaring down the road to the house.

It was my cousin, Lauralee Manning, wearing her WAVE uniform and smoking Camels in an ivory holder. Lauralee had been widowed at the beginning of the war when her young husband crashed his Navy training plane into the Pacific.

Lauralee dried her tears, joined the WAVES, and went off to avenge his death. I had not seen this paragon since I was a small child, but I had memorized the photograph Miss Onnie Maud, who was Lauralee's mother, kept on her dresser. It was a photograph of Lauralee leaning against the rail of a destroyer.

Not that Lauralee ever went to sea on a destroyer. She was spending the war in Pensacola, Florida, being secretary to an admiral.

Now, out of a clear blue sky, here was Lauralee, home on leave with a two-carat diamond ring and the news that she was getting married.

'You might have called and given some warning,' Miss Onnie Maud said, turning Lauralee into a mass of wrinkles with her embraces. 'You could have softened the blow with a letter.'

'Who's the groom?' my grandmother said. 'I only hope he's not a pilot.'

'Is he an admiral?' I said, 'or a colonel or a major or a commander?'

'My fiancé's not in uniform, Honey,' Lauralee said. 'He's in real estate. He runs the war-bond effort for the whole state of Florida. Last year he collected half a million dollars.'

'In real estate!' Miss Onnie Maud said, gasping. 'What religion is he?'

'He's Unitarian,' she said. 'His name is Donald Marcus. He's best friends with Admiral Semmes, that's how I met him. And he's coming a week from Saturday, and that's all the time we have to get ready for the wedding.'

'Unitarian!' Miss Onnie Maud said. 'I don't think I've ever met a Unitarian.'

'Why isn't he in uniform?' I insisted.

'He has flat feet,' Lauralee said gaily. 'But you'll love him when you see him.'

Later that afternoon Lauralee took me off by myself for a ride in the sedan.

'Your mother is my favorite cousin,' she said, touching my face with gentle fingers. 'You'll look just like her when you grow up and get your figure.'

I moved closer, admiring the brass buttons on her starched uniform and the brisk way she shifted and braked and put in the clutch and accelerated.

We drove down the river road and out to the bootlegger's shack where Lauralee bought a pint of Jack Daniel's and two Cokes. She poured out half of her Coke, filled it with whiskey, and we roared off down the road with the radio playing.

We drove along in the lengthening day. Lauralee was chain-smoking, lighting one Camel after another, tossing the butts out the window, taking sips from her bourbon and Coke. I sat beside her, pretending to smoke a piece of rolled-up paper, making little noises into the mouth of my Coke bottle.

We drove up to a picnic spot on the levee and sat under a tree to look out at the river.

'I miss this old river,' she said. 'When I'm sad I dream about it licking the tops of the levees.'

I didn't know what to say to that. To tell the truth I was afraid to say much of anything to Lauralee. She seemed so splendid. It was enough to be allowed to sit by her on the levee.

'Now, Rhoda,' she said, 'your mother was matron of honor in my wedding to Buddy, and I want you, her own little daughter, to be maid of honor in my second wedding.'

I could hardly believe my ears! While I was trying to think of something to say to this wonderful news I saw that Lauralee was crying, great tears were forming in her blue eyes.

'Under this very tree is where Buddy and I got engaged,' she said. Now the tears were really starting to roll, falling all over the front of her uniform. 'He gave me my ring right where we're sitting.'

'The maid of honor?' I said, patting her on the shoulder, trying to be of some comfort. 'You really mean the maid of honor?'

'Now he's gone from the world,' she continued, 'and I'm marrying a wonderful man, but that doesn't make it any easier. Oh, Rhoda, they never even found his body, never even found his body.'

I was patting her on the head now, afraid she would forget her offer in the midst of her sorrow.

'You mean I get to be the real maid of honor?'

'Oh, yes, Rhoda, Honey,' she said. 'The maid of honor, my only attendant.' She blew her nose on a lace-trimmed handkerchief and sat up straighter, taking a drink from the Coke bottle.

'Not only that, but I have decided to let you pick out your own dress. We'll go to Greenville and you can try on every dress at Nell's and Blum's and you can have the one you like the most.'

I threw my arms around her, burning with happiness, smelling her whiskey and Camels and the dark Tabu perfume that was her signature. Over her shoulder and through the low branches of the trees the afternoon sun was going down in an orgy of reds and blues and purples and violets, falling from sight, going all the way to China.

Let them keep their nasty Broad Jump Pit, I thought. Wait till they hear about this. Wait till they find out I'm maid of honor in a military wedding.

Finding the dress was another matter. Early the next morning Miss Onnie Maud and my grandmother and Lauralee and I set out for Greenville.

As we passed the pasture I hung out the back window making faces at the athletes. This time they only pretended to ignore me. They couldn't ignore this wedding. It was going to be in the parlor instead of the church so they wouldn't even get to be altar boys. They wouldn't get to light a candle.

'I don't know why you care what's going on in that pasture,' my grandmother said. 'Even if they let you play with them all it would do is make you a lot of ugly muscles.'

'Then you'd have big old ugly arms like Weegie Toler,' Miss Onnie Maude said. 'Lauralee, you remember Weegie Toler, that was a swimmer. Her arms got so big no one would take her to a dance, much less marry her.'

'Well, I don't want to get married anyway,' I said. 'I'm never getting married. I'm going to New York City and be a lawyer.'

'Where does she get those ideas?' Miss Onnie Maud said.

'When you get older you'll want to get married,' Lauralee said. 'Look at how much fun you're having being in my wedding.'

'Well, I'm never getting married,' I said. 'And I'm never having any children. I'm going to New York and be a lawyer and save people from the electric chair.'

'It's the movies,' Miss Onnie Maud said. 'They let her watch anything she likes in Indiana.'

We walked into Nell's and Blum's Department Store and took up the largest dressing-room. My grandmother and Miss Onnie Maud were seated on brocade chairs and every saleslady in the store came crowding around trying to get in on the wedding.

I refused to even consider the dresses they brought from the 'girls' ' department.

'I told her she could wear whatever she wanted,' Lauralee said, 'and I'm keeping my promise.'

'Well, she's not wearing green satin or I'm not coming,' my grandmother said, indicating the dress I had found on a rack and was clutching against me.

'At least let her try it on,' Lauralee said. 'Let her see for herself.' She zipped me into the green satin. It came down to my ankles and fit around my midsection like a girdle, making my waist seem smaller than my stomach. I admired myself in the mirror. It was almost perfect. I looked exactly like a nightclub singer.

'This one's fine,' I said. 'This is the one I want.'

'It looks marvelous, Rhoda,' Lauralee said, 'but it's the wrong color for the wedding. Remember I'm wearing blue.'

'I believe the child's colour-blind,' Miss Onnie Maud said. 'It runs in her father's family.

'I am not colour-blind,' I said, reaching behind me and unzipping the dress. 'I have twenty-twenty vision.'

'Let her try on some more,' Lauralee said. 'Let her try on everything in the store.'

I proceeded to do just that, with the salesladies getting grumpier and grumpier. I tried on a gold gabardine dress with a rhinestone-studded cummerbund. I tried on a pink ballerina-length formal and a lavender voile tea dress and several silk suits. Somehow nothing looked right.

'Maybe we'll have to make her something,' my grandmother said.

'But there's no time,' Miss Onnie Maud said. 'Besides first we'd have to find out what she wants. Rhoda, please tell us what you're looking for.'

Their faces all turned to mine, waiting for an answer. But I didn't know the answer.

The dress I wanted was a secret. The dress I wanted was dark and tall and thin as a reed. There was a word for what I wanted, a word I had seen in magazines. But what was that word? I could not remember.

'I want something dark,' I said at last. 'Something dark and silky.'

'Wait right there,' the saleslady said. 'Wait just a minute.' Then, from out of a pre-war storage closet she brought a black-watch plaid recital dress with spaghetti straps and a white piqué jacket. It was made of taffeta and rustled when I touched it. There was a label sewn into the collar of the jacket. *Little Miss Sophisticate*, it said. *Sophisticate*, that was the word I was seeking.

I put on the dress and stood triumphant in a sea of ladies and dresses and hangers.

'This is the dress,' I said. 'This is the dress I'm wearing.'

'It's perfect,' Lauralee said. 'Start hemming it up. She'll be the prettiest maid of honor in the whole world.'

All the way home I held the box on my lap thinking about how I would look in the dress. Wait till they see me like this, I was thinking. Wait till they see what I really look like.

I fell in love with the groom. The moment I laid eyes on him I forgot he was flat-footed. He arrived bearing gifts of music and perfume and candy, a warm dark-skinned man with eyes the color of walnuts.

He laughed out loud when he saw me, standing on the porch with my hands on my hips.

'This must be Rhoda,' he exclaimed, 'the famous red-haired maid of honor.' He came running up the steps, gave me a slow, exciting hug, and presented me with a whole album of Xavier Cugat records. I had never owned a record of my own, much less an album.

Before the evening was over I put on a red formal I found in a trunk and did a South American dance for him to Xavier Cugat's 'Poinciana'. He said he had never seen anything like it in his whole life.

The wedding itself was a disappointment. No one came but the immediate family and there was no aisle to march down and the only music was Onnie Maud playing 'Liebestraum.'

Dudley and Philip and Saint John and Oliver and Bunky were dressed in long pants and white shirts and ties. They had fresh military crew cuts and looked like a nest of new birds, huddled together on the blue velvet sofa, trying to keep their hands to themselves, trying to figure out how to act at a wedding.

The elderly Episcopal priest read out the ceremony in a gravelly smoker's voice, ruining all the good parts by coughing. He was in a bad mood because Lauralee and Mr Marcus hadn't found time to come to him for marriage instruction.

Still, I got to hold the bride's flowers while he gave her the ring and stood so close to her during the ceremony I could hear her breathing.

The reception was better. People came from all over the Delta. There were tables with candles set up around the porches and sprays of greenery in every corner. There were gentlemen sweating in linen suits and the record-player playing every minute. In the back hall Calvin had set up a real professional bar with tall, permanently-frosted glasses and ice and mint and lemons and every kind of whiskey and liqueur in the world.

I stood in the receiving line getting compliments on my dress, then wandered around the rooms eating cake and letting people hug me. After a while I got bored with that and went out to the back hall and began to fix myself a drink at the bar.

I took one of the frosted glasses and began filling it from different bottles, tasting as I went along. I used plenty of crème de menthe and soon had something that tasted heavenly. I filled the glass with crushed ice, added three straws, and went out to sit on the back steps and cool off.

I was feeling wonderful. A full moon was caught like a kite in the pecan trees across the river. I sipped along on my drink. Then, without planning it, I did something I had never dreamed of doing. I left the porch alone at night. Usually I was in terror of the dark. My grandmother had told me that alligators come out of the bayou to eat children who wander alone at night.

I walked out across the yard, the huge moon giving so much light I almost cast a shadow. When I was nearly to the water's edge I turned and looked back toward the house. It shimmered in the moonlight like a juke-box alive in a meadow, seemed to pulsate with music and laughter and people, beautiful and foreign, not a part of me.

I looked out at the water, then down the road to the pasture. The Broad Jump Pit! There it was, perfect and unguarded. Why had I never thought of doing this before?

I began to run toward the road. I ran as fast as my Mary Jane pumps would allow me. I pulled my dress up around my waist and climbed the fence in one motion, dropping lightly down on the other side. I was sweating heavily, alone with the moon and my wonderful courage.

I knew exactly what to do first. I picked up the pole and hoisted it over my head. It felt solid and balanced and alive. I hoisted it up and down a few times as I had seen Dudley do, getting the feel of it.

Then I laid it ceremoniously down on the ground, reached

behind me, and unhooked the plaid formal. I left it lying in a heap on the ground. There I stood, in my cotton underpants, ready to take up pole-vaulting.

I lifted the pole and carried it back to the end of the cinder path. I ran slowly down the path, stuck the pole in the wooden cup, and attempted throwing my body into the air, using it as a lever.

Something was wrong. It was more difficult than it appeared from a distance. I tried again. Nothing happened. I sat down with the pole across my legs to think things over.

Then I remembered something I had watched Dudley doing through the binoculars. He measured down from the end of the pole with his fingers spread wide. That was it, I had to hold it closer to the end.

I tried it again. This time the pole lifted me several feet off the ground. My body sailed across the grass in a neat arc and I landed on my toes. I was a natural!

I do not know how long I was out there, running up and down the cinder path, thrusting my body further and further through space, tossing myself into the pit like a mussel shell thrown across the bayou.

At last I decided I was ready for the real test. I had to vault over a cane barrier. I examined the pegs on the wooden poles and chose one that came up to my shoulder.

I put the barrier pole in place, spit over my left shoulder, and marched back to the end of the path. Suck up your guts, I told myself. It's only a pole. It won't get stuck in your stomach and tear out your insides. It won't kill you.

I stood at the end of the path eyeballing the barrier. Then, above the incessant racket of the crickets, I heard my name being called. Rhoda ... the voices were calling. Rhoda ... Rhoda ... Rhoda ... Rhoda.

I turned toward the house and saw them coming. Mr Marcus and Dudley and Bunky and Calvin and Lauralee and what looked like half the wedding. They were climbing the fence, calling my name, and coming to get me. Rhoda ... they called out. Where on earth have you been? What on earth are you doing?

I hoisted the pole up to my shoulders and began to run down the path, running into the light from the moon. I picked up speed, thrust the pole into the cup, and threw myself into the sky, into the still Delta night. I sailed up and was clear and over the barrier.

I let go of the pole and began my fall, which seemed to last a long, long time. It was like falling through clear water. I dropped into the sawdust and lay very still, waiting for them to reach me.

Sometimes I think whatever has happened since has been of no real interest to me.

Girl

Jamaica Kincaid

Wash the white clothes on Monday and and put them on the
stone heap; wash the color clothes on Tuesday and put them
on the clothes-line to dry; don't walk barehead in the hot sun;
cook pumpkin fritters in very hot sweet oil; soak your little cloths
right after you take them off; when buying cotton to make
yourself a nice blouse, be sure that it doesn't have gum on it,
because that way it won't hold up well after a wash; soak salt fish
over night before you cook it; is it true that you sing benna in
Sunday school?; always eat your food in such a way that it won't
turn someone else's stomach; on Sundays try to walk like a lady
and not like the slut you are so bent on becoming; don't sing
benna in Sunday school; you mustn't speak to wharf-rat boys,
not even to give directions; don't eat fruits on the street – flies
will follow you; *but I don't sing benna on Sundays at all and never in
Sunday school;* this is how to sew on a button; this is how to hem a
dress when you see the hem coming down and so to prevent
yourself from looking like the slut I know you are so bent on
becoming; this is how you iron your father's khaki shirt so that it
doesn't have a crease; this is how you iron your father's khaki
pants so that they don't have a crease; this is how you grow okra
– far from the house, because okra tree harbors red ants; when
you are growing dasheen, make sure it gets plenty of water or
else it makes your throat itch when you are eating it; this is how
you sweep a corner; this is how you sweep a whole house; this is
how you sweep a yard; this is how you smile to someone you
don't like too much; this is how you smile to someone you don't
like at all; this is how you smile to someone you like completely;
this is how you set a table for tea; this is how you set a table for
dinner; this is how you set a table for dinner with an important
guest; this is how you set a table for lunch; this is how you set a

table for breakfast; this is how to behave in the presence of men who don't know you very well, and this way they won't recognize immediately the slut I have warned you against becoming; be sure to wash every day, even if it is with your own spit; don't squat down to play marbles – you are not a boy, you know; don't pick people's flowers – you might catch something; don't throw stones at blackbirds, because it might not be a blackbird at all; this is how to make a bread pudding; this is how to make doukona; this is how to make pepper pot; this is how to make a good medicine for a cold; this is how to make a good medicine to throw away a child before it even becomes a child; this is how to catch a fish; this is how to throw back a fish you don't like, and that way something bad won't fall on you; this is how to bully a man; this is how a man bullies you; this is how to love a man, and if this doesn't work there are other ways, and if they don't work don't feel too bad about giving up; this is how to spit up in the air if you feel like it, and this is how to move quick so that it doesn't fall on you; this is how to make ends meet; always squeeze bread to make sure it's fresh; *but what if the baker won't let me feel the bread?*; you mean to say that after all you are really going to be the kind of woman who the baker won't let near the bread?

Sweet Sixteen

Michelene Wandor

Sixteen soft pink blankets fold inwards over sixteen soft warm smiling babies. Sixteen dark-haired young mothers meet their sixteen babies' soft smiling mouths in a kiss. Sixteen mothers and babies recede into the soft-focus blues and greens of sixteen immaculate gardens.

Naomi looks round to see the cluster of other mothers, like herself, mesmerized by Granada TV Rental's windows. The mothers swap little grins and turn their attention back to the real babies bundled in push-chairs and prams. The cluster breaks, and its various components span out across the cool marble floor, past the glass and perspex walls, through the chrome and glass doors and into the world of echoing footsteps, surrounding arcades and fountains and climbing and weeping shrubbery.

Lucy strains to stand up in her push-chair. Naomi eases her out of the canvas straps and settles her on the red seat of the silver trolley. She pauses momentarily, to decide which is to be the first aisle of the journey; should she start with soft drinks, vegetables, frozen foods, tins – she decides on fruit juice. As they wheel past the rack of special-offer Mars bars, Naomi gently deflects Lucy's outstretched hand, her thumb briefly stroking the soft palm of Lucy's hand. I could do the shopping with my eyes shut, thinks Naomi, once a week for how many weeks, everything always in the same place. She turns the trolley to the right, to the fridge where the pineapple juice cartons – she stops. The open maw of the fridge gapes. It is empty. Ah well. Perhaps they have run out of cartons of fruit juice.

She decides to do dairy products next; cream, butter, some yoghurt – but instead, on the racks where the dairy products used to be, she finds pizzas, steak and kidney pies in coy transparent wrappings, and further on packets of frozen, sleeping raspberries and apple and blackberry crumbles. Something is wrong. She begins to collect, feeling uneasy that it isn't in the order of her choice, worried that if she leaves things now to go on to another aisle, they will have disappeared when she gets back.

She wheels on, to where she expects to find the vegetable racks: the net bags of French apples, the South African avocados, severely boycotted each time. But instead there are long blue and red spaghetti packets, rice, curled dusty pasta. Again she collects, panic beginning to rise. She mustn't show it to Lucy, who is happy being wheeled at such sight-seeing speed, happy to have her outstretched hand denied, because her desire is being stroked at the rate of new products every thirty seconds.

Naomi makes confidently for the cold meat counter, it is dark, piled up with unattended towers of soft toilet paper; the plastic box where scraps of meat were sold cheaply, the ends of cuts, is upside down, empty. For the first time she notices the other women. They walk fast, their heads slightly bent, cradling high-piled baskets, anxiety on their faces, grabbing cereals, bread, soap powders, cleansers, hurrying past pensioners, skirting toddlers, running, running.

Lucy now has a fist in her mouth, enjoying the game, enjoying the deftness of the domestic dodgems where years of unthinking practice has enabled the women to anticipate corners, come to a full stop at the precise point of need, to turn in a tight space, to avoid and yet not slacken speed. Naomi speeds up to join the pace, taking what she can wherever she can, until she arrives at the back of the floor space, at the point where the soft drinks used to be. Naomi gasps. The once smooth space is now a raw gash, copper cables twisting like thick muscle fibre, clinging to the broken brick and plaster gaps in the walls.

Naomi hears a voice saying, Nothing is where it was. Lucy giggles and she realizes that she has spoken out loud. She looks round. No one seems to have heard her. They are all too busy. Naomi looks down at the trolley. It is full of everything she has meant to buy, but none of it is in the right order, the order she is used to.

Naomi wheels the trolley slowly towards the cash tills. Lucy, sensitive to the change in pace, stops giggling; she is now pale and still. Naomi joins a queue at a cash till, watching the other women, their eyes darting, their hands cupped protectively over their prospective purchases, as if there were some danger of someone whisking everything out again and back onto the alien shelves.

Naomi stands behind a woman who fumbles for her cheque-book. Naomi watches as the white snakes with purple figures spill out of the tills, paper bags, plastic carriers, boxes and baskets flash between the tills and the plate glass window.

Naomi's turn comes. She lifts a bottle of lemon and lime out of the trolley. The outside is sticky. Naomi moves her index and second fingers to a dry part of the bottle, her hand slips, the bottle falls, its soft edge knocks against the rim of the conveyor belt and bursts.

Thick, bright green liquid squirts luminously back into the trolley, over tins of tuna fish. Lucy claps her hands in delight, and reaching into the trolley, she lifts a packet of white self-raising flour and drops it with a dull thud on the floor. A white cloud powders the feet of the women. Lucy giggles. Naomi feels a cloud of answering laughter rise in her, tries to keep it down, looks up and catches the eye of the woman queuing behind her. The woman smiles, ruffles Lucy's hair and then lifts a bag of tomatoes from her own basket and hurls it overarm against the special offer of tea bags. Red seed drips down against the green boxes.

The women look at one other. Suddenly bits of flattened, squared ham fly free of their jellied, cellophane packets, duck pâté bursts out of its blue pottery bowls, salt and vinegar crisps crackle underfoot, sliding through whiter than white cottage cheese, a treacle pudding roosts among the spilled biscuit crumbs. The air is thick with suspended golden arcs from tinned peaches, rains of mint-flavoured petit pois, chunky Branston pickle washed along by mineral water from Malvern spa.

The lights of the cash tills spark white, the women sitting at the money machines aren't sure which way to turn, one surreptitiously picks up a cucumber and slides it along the floor, into a welcoming pool of raspberry yoghurt.

Outside the plate glass window red and blue lights flash as pale men in dark blue peer through the window at all the Christmas and birthday and anniversary celebrations in one.

Ten feet away, sixteen dark-haired mothers smile at their babies for the sixteenth time and enfold them in sixteen warm, pink blankets.

Queen for a Day

Russell Banks

The elder of the two boys, Earl, turns from the dimly-lit worktable, a door on sawhorses, where he is writing. He pauses a second and says to his brother, 'Cut that out, willya? Getcha feet off the walls.'

The other boy says, 'Don't tell me what to do. You're not the boss of this family, you know.' He is dark-haired with large brown eyes, a moody ten-year-old lying bored on his cot with sneakered feet slapped against the faded green floral print wallpaper.

Earl crosses his arms over his bony chest and stares down at his brother from a considerable height. The room is cluttered with model airplanes, schoolbooks, papers, clothing, hockey-sticks and skates, a set of barbells. Earl says, 'We're supposed to be doing homework, you know. If she hears you tramping your feet on the walls, she'll come in here screaming. So get your damned feet off the wall. I ain't kidding.'

'She can't hear me. Besides, you ain't doing homework. And *I'm* reading,' he says, waving a geography book at him.

The older boy sucks his breath through his front teeth and glares. 'You really piss me off, George. Just put your god-damned feet down, will you? I can't concentrate with you doing that, rubbing your feet all over the wallpaper like you're doing. It makes me all distracted.' He turns back to his writing, scribbling with a ballpoint pen on lined paper in a schoolboy's three-ring binder. Earl has sandy blond hair and pale blue eyes that turn downward at the corners and a full red mouth. He's more scrawny than skinny, hard and flat-muscled, and suddenly tall for his age, making him a head taller than his brother, taller even than their mother now, too, and able to pat their sister's head as if he were a full-grown adult already.

He turned twelve eight months ago, in March, and in May

their father left. Their father is a union carpenter who works on projects in distant corners of the state – schools, hospitals, post offices – and for a whole year the man came home only on weekends. Then, for a while, every other weekend. Finally, he was gone for a month, and when he came home the last time, it was to say goodbye to Earl, George, and their sister Louise, and to their mother, too, of course, she who had been saying (for what seemed to the children years) that she never wanted to see the man again anyhow, ever, under any circumstances, because he just causes trouble when he's home and more trouble when he doesn't come home, so he might as well stay away for good. They can all get along better without him, she insisted, which was true, Earl was sure, but that was before the man left for good and stopped sending them money, so that now, six months later, Earl is not so sure anymore that they can get along better without their father than with him.

It happened on a Sunday morning, a day washed with new sunshine and dry air, with the whole family standing sombrely in the kitchen, summoned there from their rooms by their mother's taut, high-pitched voice, a voice that had an awful point to prove. 'Come out here! Your father has something important to say to you!'

They obeyed, one by one, and gathered in a line before their father, who, dressed in pressed khakis and shined work shoes and cap, sat at the kitchen table, a pair of suitcases beside him, and in front of him a cup of coffee, which he stirred slowly with a spoon. His eyes were red and filled with dense water, the way they almost always were on Sunday mornings, from his drinking the night before, the children knew, and he had trouble looking them in the face, because of the sorts of things he and their mother were heard saying to one another when they were at home together late Saturday nights. On this Sunday morning it was only a little worse than usual – his hands shook some, and he could barely hold his cigarette; he let it smoulder in the ashtray and kept on stirring his coffee while he talked. 'Your mother and me,' he said in his low, roughened voice, 'we've decided on some things you kids should know about.' He cleared his throat. 'Your mother, she thinks you oughta hear it from me, though I don't quite know so much about that as she does, since it isn't completely my idea alone.' He studied his coffee cup for a few seconds.

'They should hear it from you because it's what you *want!*' their mother finally said. She stood by the sink, her hands wringing each other dry, and stared over at the man. Her face was swollen and red from crying, which, for the children, was not an unusual thing to see on a Sunday morning when their father was home. They still did not know what was coming.

'Adele, it's *not* what I want,' he said. 'It's what's got to be, that's all. Kids,' he said, 'I got to leave you folks for a while. A long while. And I won't be comin' back, I guess.' He grabbed his cigarette with thumb and forefinger and inhaled the smoke fiercely, then placed the butt back into the ashtray and went on talking, as if to the table: 'I don't want to do this, I hate it, but I got to. It's too hard to explain, and I'm hoping that someday you'll understand it all, but I just ... I just got to live somewheres else now.'

Louise, the little girl, barely six years old, was the only one of the three children who could speak. She said, 'Where are you going, Daddy?'

'Upstate,' he said. 'Back up to Holderness, where I been all along. I got me an apartment up there, small place.'

'That's not all he's got up there!' their mother said.

'Adele, I can walk outa here right this second,' he said smoothly. 'I don't hafta explain a damned thing, if you keep that kinda stuff up. We had an agreement.'

'Yup, yup. Sorry,' she said, pursing her lips, locking them with an invisible key, throwing the key away.

Finally, Earl could speak. 'Will ... will you come and see us, or can we come visit you, on weekends and like that?' he asked his father.

'Sure, son, you can visit me, anytime you want. It'll take a while for me to get the place set up right, but soon's I get it all set up for kids, I'll call you, and we'll work out some nice visits. I shouldn't come here, though, not for a while. You understand.'

Earl shook his head sombrely up and down, as if his one anxiety concerning this event had been put satisfactorily to rest.

George had turned his back on his father, however, and now he was taking tiny, mincing half-steps across the linoleum-covered kitchen floor toward the outside door. Then he stopped a second, opened the door and stood on the landing at the top of the stairs, and no one tried to stop him, because he was doing what they wanted to do themselves, and then they heard him running pell-mell, as if falling, down the darkened stairs, two flights, to the front door of the building, heard it slam behind him, and knew he was gone, up Perley Street, between parked cars, down alleys, to a hiding place where they knew he'd stop, sit, and bawl, knew it because it was what they wanted to do themselves, especially Earl, who was too old, too scared, too confused and too angry. Instead of running away and bawling, Earl said, 'I hope everyone can be more happy now.'

His father smiled and looked at him for the first time and clapped him on the shoulder. 'Hey, son,' he said, 'you, you're the man of the house now. I know you can do it. You're a good kid, and listen, I'm proud of you. Your mother, your brother and sister, they're all going to need you a hell of a lot more than they have before, but I know you're up to it, son. I'm countin' on ya,' he said, and he stood up and rubbed out his cigarette. Then he reached beyond Earl with both hands and hugged Earl's little sister, lifted her off her feet and squeezed her tight, and when the man set her down, he wiped tears away from his eyes. 'Tell Georgie . . . well, maybe I'll see him downstairs or something. He's upset, I guess . . .' He shook Earl's hand, drew him close, quickly hugged him and let go and stepped away. Grabbing up his suitcases, in silence, without looking over once at his wife or back at his children, he left the apartment.

For good. 'And good riddance, too,' as their mother immediately started saying to anyone who would listen. Louise said she missed her daddy, but she seemed to be quickly forgetting that, since for most of her life he had worked away from home, and George, who stayed mad, went deep inside himself and said nothing about it at all, and Earl – who did not know how he felt about their father's abandoning them, for he knew that in many ways it was the best their father could do for them and in many other ways it was the worst – spoke of the man as if he had died in an accident, as if their mother were a widow and they half orphaned. This freed him, though he did not know it then, to concentrate on survival, survival for them all, which he now understood to be his personal responsibility, for his mother seemed utterly incapable of guaranteeing it and his brother and sister, of course, were still practically babies. Often, late at night, lying in his squeaky, narrow cot next to his brother's, Earl would say to himself, 'I'm the man of the house now,' and somehow just saying it, over and over, 'I'm the man of the house now,' like a prayer, made his terror ease back away from his face, and he could finally slip into sleep.

Now, with his father gone six months and their mother still fragile, still denouncing the man to everyone who listens, and even to those who don't listen but merely show her their faces for a moment or two, it's as if the man were still coming home weekends drunk and raging against her and the world, were still betraying her, were telling all her secrets to another woman in a motel room in the northern part of the state. It's as if he were daily abandoning her and their three children over and over again, agreeing to send money and then sending nothing, promising to call and write letters and then going silent on them, planning visits and trips together on weekends and holidays and then leaving them with not even a forwarding address, forbidding them, almost, from adjusting to a new life, a life in which their father and her husband does not betray them anymore.

Earl decides to solve their problems himself. He hatches and implements, as best he can, plans, schemes, designs, all intended to find a substitute for the lost father. He introduces his mother to his hockey coach, who turns out to be married and a new father; and he invites in for breakfast and to meet his ma the cigar-smoking vet with the metal plate in his skull who drops off the newspapers at dawn for Earl to deliver before school, but the man turns out to dislike women actively enough to tell Earl so, right to his face: 'No offense, kid, I'm sure your ma's a nice lady, but I got no use for 'em is why I'm single, not 'cause I ain't met the right one yet or something'; and to the guy who comes to read the electric meter one afternoon when Earl's home from school with the flu and his mother's at work down at the tannery, where they've taken her on as an assistant bookkeeper, Earl says that he can't let the man into the basement because it's locked and he'll have to come back later when his mom's home, so she can let him in herself, and the man says, 'Hey, no problem, I can use last month's reading and make the correction next month,' and waves cheerfully goodbye, leaving Earl suddenly, utterly, shockingly aware of his foolishness, his pathetic, helpless longing for a man of the house.

For a moment, he blames his mother for his longing and hates her for his fantasies. But then quickly he forgives her and blames himself and commences to concoct what he thinks of as more realistic, more dignified plans, schemes, designs: sweepstakes tickets, lotteries, raffles – Earl buys tickets on the sly with his paper route money. And he enters contests, essay contests for junior high school students that provide the winner with a week-long trip for him and a parent to Washington D.C., and the National Spelling Bee, which takes Earl only to the county level before he fails to spell 'alligator' correctly. A prize, any kind of award from the world outside their tiny, besieged family, Earl believes, will validate their new life somehow and will thus separate it, once and for all, from their father. It will be as if their father never existed.

'So what are you writing now?' George demands from the bed. He walks his feet up the wall as high as he can reach, then retreats. 'I know it ain't homework, you don't write that fast when you're doing homework. What is it, a *love* letter?' He leers.

'No, asshole. Just take your damned feet off the wall, will you? Ma's gonna be in here in a minute screaming at both of us.' Earl closes the notebook and pushes it away from him carefully, as if it is the Bible and he has just finished reading aloud from it.

'I wanna see what you wrote,' George says, flipping around and setting his feet, at last, onto the floor. He reaches toward the notebook. 'Lemme see it.'

'C'mon, willya? Cut the shit.'

'Naw, lemme see it.' He stands up and swipes the notebook from the table as Earl moves to protect it.

'You little sonofabitch!' Earl says, and he clamps onto the notebook with both hands and yanks, pulling George off his feet and forward onto Earl's lap, and they both tumble to the floor, where they begin to fight, swing fists and knees, roll and grab, bumping against furniture in the tiny, crowded room, until a lamp falls over, books tumble to the floor, model airplanes crash. In seconds, George is getting the worst of it and scrambles across the floor to the door, with Earl crawling along behind, yanking his brother's shirt with one hand and pounding at his head and back with the other, when suddenly the bedroom door swings open, and their mother stands over them. Grabbing both boys by their collars, she shrieks, 'What's the matter with you! What're you doing! What're you doing!' They stop and collapse into a bundle of legs and arms, but she goes on shrieking at them. 'I can't *stand* it when you fight! Don't you know that? I can't *stand* it!'

George cries, 'I didn't do anything! I just wanted to see his homework!'

'Yeah, sure,' Earl says. 'Sure. Innocent as a baby.'

'Shut up! Both of you!' their mother screams. She is wild-eyed, glaring down at them, and, as he has done so many times, Earl looks at her face as if he's outside his body, and he sees that she's not angry at them at all, she's frightened and in pain, as if her sons are little animals, rats or ferrets, with tiny, razor-sharp teeth biting at her ankles and feet.

Quickly, Earl gets to his feet and says, 'I'm sorry, Ma. I guess I'm just a little tired or something lately.' He pats his mother on her shoulder and offers a small smile. George crawls on hands and knees back to his bed and lies on it, while Earl gently turns their mother around and steers her back out the door to the living-room, where the television set drones on, Les Paul and Mary Ford, playing their guitars and singing bland harmonies. 'We'll be out in a few minutes for *Dobie Gillis*, Ma. Don't worry,' Earl says.

'Jeez,' George says. 'How can she stand that Les Paul and Mary Ford stuff? Yuck. Even Louise goes to bed when it comes on, and it's only what, six-thirty?'

'Yeah. Shut up.'

'Up yours.'

Earl leans down and scoops up the fallen dictionary, pens, airplanes and lamp and places them back on the work-table. The black binder he opens squarely in front of him, and he says to his brother, 'Here, you wanta see what I was writing? Go ahead and read it. I don't care.'

'I don't care, either. Unless it's a *love* letter!'

'No, it's not a *love* letter.'

'What is it, then?'

'Nothing,' Earl says, closing the notebook. 'Homework.'

'Oh,' George says, and he starts marching his feet up the wall and back again.

Nov. 7, 1953

Dear Jack Bailey,

     I think my mother should be queen for a day because she has suffered a lot more than most mothers in this life and she has come out of it very cheerful and loving. The most important fact is that my father left her alone with three children, myself (age 12½), my brother George (age 10), and my sister Louise (age 6). He left her for another woman though that's not the important thing, because my mother has risen above all that. But he refuses to send her any child support money. He's been gone over six months and we still haven't seen one cent. My mother went to a lawyer but the lawyer wants $50 in advance to help her take my father to court. She has a job as assistant bookkeeper down at Belvedere's Tannery downtown and the pay is bad, barely enough for our rent and food costs in fact, so where is she going to get $50 for a lawyer?

     Also my father was a very cruel man who drinks too much and many times when he was living with us when he came home from work he was drunk and he would beat her.

This has caused her and us kids a lot of nervous suffering and now she sometimes has spells which the doctor says are serious, though he doesn't know exactly what they are.

We used to have a car and my father left it with us when he left (a big favor) because he had a pickup truck. But he owed over $450 on the car to the bank so the bank came and repossessed the car. Now my mother has to walk everywhere she goes which is hard and causes her varicose veins and takes a lot of valuable time from her day.

My sister Louise needs glasses the school nurse said but 'Who can pay for them?' my mother says. My paper route gets a little money but it's barely enough for school lunches for the three of us kids which is what we use it for.

My mother's two sisters and her brother haven't been too helpful because they are Catholic, as she is and the rest of us, and they don't believe in divorce and think that she should not have let my father leave her anyhow. She needs to get a divorce but no one except me and my brother George think it is a good idea. Therefore my mother cries a lot at night because she feels so abandoned in this time of her greatest need.

The rest of the time though she is cheerful and loving in spite of her troubles and nervousness. That is why I believe that this courageous long-suffering woman, my mother, should be Queen for a Day.

> Sincerely yours,
> Earl Painter

Several weeks slide by, November gets cold and gray, and a New Hampshire winter starts to feel inevitable again, and Earl does not receive the letter he expects. He has told no one, especially his mother, that he has written to Jack Bailey, the smiling, mustachioed host of the *Queen for a Day* television show, which Earl happened to see that time he was home for several days with the flu, bored and watching television all afternoon. Afterwards, delivering papers in the predawn gloom, in school all day, at the hockey rink, doing homework at night, he could not forget about the television show, the sad stories told by the contestants about their illness, poverty, neglect, victimization and, always, their bad luck, luck so bad that you feel it's somehow deserved. The studio audience seemed genuinely saddened, moved to tears, even, by Jack Bailey's recitation of these narratives, and then elated afterwards, when the winning victims, all of them middle-aged women, were rewarded with refrigerators, living-room suites, vacation trips, washing-machines, china, fur coats and, if they needed them, wheel-chairs, prosthetic limbs, twenty-four-hour nursing care. As these women wept for joy, the audience applauded, and Earl almost applauded too, alone there in the dim living-room of the small, cold, and threadbare apartment in a mill town in central New Hampshire.

Earl knows that those women's lives surely aren't much different from his mother's life, and in fact, if he has told it right, if somehow he has got into the letter what he has intuited is basically wrong with his mother's life, it will be obvious to everyone in the audience that his mother's life is actually much worse than that of many or perhaps even most of the women who win the prizes. Earl knows that though his mother enjoys good health (except for 'spells') and holds down a job and is able to feed, house, and clothe her children, there is still a deep, essential sadness in her life that, in his eyes, none of the contestants on *Queen for a Day* has. He believes that if he can just get his description of her life right, other people – Jack Bailey, the studio audience, millions of people all over America watching it on television – *everyone* will share in her sadness, so that when she is rewarded with appliances, furniture and clothing, maybe even a trip to Las Vegas, then everyone will share in her elation, too. Even he will share in it.

Earl knows that it is not easy to become a contestant on *Queen for a Day*. Somehow your letter describing the candidate has first to move Jack Bailey, and then your candidate has to be able to communicate her sufferings over television in a clear and dramatic way. Earl noticed that some of the contestants, to their own apparent disadvantage, down-played the effect on them of certain tragedies – a child with a birth defect, say, or an embarrassing kind of operation or a humiliating dismissal by an employer – while playing up other, seemingly less disastrous events, such as being cheated out of a small inheritance by a phony siding contractor or having to drop out of hairdressing school because of a parent's illness, and when the studio audience was asked to show the extent and depth of its compassion by having its applause measured on a meter, it was always the woman who managed to present the most convincing mixture of courage and complaint who won.

Earl supposes that what happens is that Jack Bailey writes or maybe telephones the writer of the letter nominating a particular woman for *Queen for a Day* and offers him and his nominee the opportunity to come to New York City's Radio City Music Hall to tell her story in person, and then, based on how she does in the audition, Jack Bailey chooses her and two other nominees for a particular show, maybe next week, when they all come back to New York City to tell their stories live on television. Thus, daily, when Earl arrives home, he asks Louise and George, who normally get home from school an hour or so earlier than he, if there's any mail for him, any letter. You're sure? Nothing? No phone calls, either?

'Who're you expectin' to hear from, lover boy, your *girl* friend?' George grins, teeth spotted with peanut butter and gobs of white bread.

'Up yours,' Earl says, and heads into his bedroom, where he dumps his coat, books, hockey gear. It's becoming clear to him that if there's such a thing as a success, he's evidently a failure. If there's such a thing as a winner, he's a loser. I oughta go on that goddamned show myself, he thinks. Flopping onto his bed face-first, he wishes he could keep on falling, as if down a bottomless well or mine shaft, into darkness and warmth, lost and finally blameless, gone, gone, gone. And soon he is asleep, dreaming of a hockey game, and he's carrying the puck, dragging it all the way up along the right, digging in close to the boards, skate blades lashing as he cuts around behind the net, ice chips spraying in white fantails, and when he comes out on the other side, he looks down in front of him and can't find the puck, it's gone, dropped off behind him, lost in his sweeping turn, the spray, the slash of the skates and the long sweeping arc of the stick in front of him. He brakes, turns, and heads back, searching for the small black disk.

At the sound of the front door closing, a quiet click, as if someone is deliberately trying to enter the apartment silently, Earl wakes from his dream, and he hears voices from the kitchen, George and Louise and his mother:

'Hi, Mom. We're just makin' a snack, peanut butter sandwiches.'

'Mommy, George won't give me – '

'Don't eat it directly off the knife like that!'

'Sorry, I was just – '

'You heard me, mister, don't answer back!'

'Jeez, I was just – '

'I don't *care* what you were doing!' Her voice is trembling and quickly rising in pitch and timbre, and Earl moves off his bed and comes into the kitchen, smiling, drawing everyone's attention to him, the largest person in the room, the only one with a smile on his face, a relaxed, easy, sociable face and manner, normalcy itself, as he gives his brother's shoulder a fraternal squeeze, tousles his sister's brown hair, nods hello to his mother and says, 'Hey, you're home early, Ma. What happened, they give you guys the rest of the day off?'

Then he sees her face, white, tight, drawn back in a cadaverous grimace, her pale blue eyes wild, unfocused, rolling back, and he says, 'Jeez, Ma, what's the matter, you okay?'

Her face breaks into pieces, goes from dry to wet, white to red, and she is weeping loudly, blubbering, wringing her hands in front of her like a maddened knitter. 'Aw-w-w-w!' she wails, and Louise and George, too, start to cry. They run to her and wrap her in their arms, crying and begging her not to cry, as Earl, aghast, sits back in his chair and watches the three of them wind around each other like snakes moving in and out of one another's coils.

'Stop!' he screams at last. 'Stop it! All of you!' He pounds his fists on the table. 'Stop crying, all of you!'

And they obey him, George first, then their mother, then Louise, who goes on staring into her mother's face. George looks at his feet, ashamed, and their mother looks pleadingly into Earl's face, expectant, hopeful, as if knowing that he will organize everything.

In a calm voice, Earl says, 'Ma, tell me what happened. Just say it slowly, you know, and it'll come out okay, and then we can all talk about it, okay?'

She nods, and slowly George unravels his arms from around her neck and steps away from her, moving to the far wall of the room, where he stands and looks out the window and down to the bare yard below. Louise snuggles her face in close to her mother and sniffles quietly.

'I . . . I lost my job. I got fired today,' their mother says. 'And it wasn't my fault,' she says, starting to weep again, and Louise joins her, bawling now, and George at the window starts to sob, his small shoulders heaving.

Earl shouts, 'Wait! Wait a minute, Ma, just *tell* me about it. Don't cry!' he commands her, and she shudders, draws herself together again and continues.

'I . . . I had some problems this morning, a bunch of files I was supposed to put away last week sometime got lost. And everybody was running around like crazy looking for them, 'cause they had all these figures from last year's sales in 'em or something, I don't know. Anyhow, they were important, and I was the one who was accused of losing them. Which I didn't! But no one could find them, until finally they turned up on Robbie's desk, down in shipping, which I couldna done since I never go to shipping anyhow. But just the same, Rose blamed me, because she's the head bookkeeper and she was the last person to use the files, and she was getting it because they needed them upstairs, and . . . well, you know, I was just getting yelled at and yelled at, and it went on after lunch . . . and, I don't know, I just started feeling dizzy and all, you know, like I was going to black out again? And I guess I got scared and started talking real fast, so Rose took me down to the nurse, and I did black out then. Only for a few seconds, though, and when I felt a little better, Rose said maybe I should go home for the rest of the day, which is what I wanted to do anyhow. But when I went back upstairs to get my pocketbook and coat and my lunch, because I hadn't been able to eat my sandwich, even, I was so nervous and all, and then Mr Shandy called me into his office . . . ' She makes a twisted little smile, helpless and confused, and quickly continues. 'Mr Shandy said I should maybe take a lot of time off. Two weeks sick leave with pay, he said, even though I was only working there six months. He said that would give me time to look for another job, one that wouldn't cause me so much worry, he said. So I said, "Are you firing me?" and he said, "Yes, I am," just like that. "But it would be better for you all around," he said, "if you left for medical reasons or something." '

Earl slowly exhales. He's been holding his breath throughout, though from her very first sentence he has known what the outcome would be. Reaching forward, he takes his mother's hands in his, stroking them as if they were an injured bird. He doesn't know what will happen now, but somehow he is not afraid. Not really. Yet he knows that he should be terrified, and when he says this to himself, *I should be terrified*, he answers by observing simply that this is not the worst thing. The worst thing that can happen to them is that one or all of them will die. And because he is still a child, or at least enough of a child not to believe in death, he knows that no one in his family is going to die. He cannot share this secret comfort with anyone in the family, however. His brother and sister, children completely, cannot yet know that death is the worst thing that can happen to them; they think this is, that their mother has been fired from her job, which is why they are crying. And his mother, no longer a child at all, cannot believe with Earl that the worst thing will not happen, for this is too much like death and may somehow lead directly to it, which is why she is crying. Only Earl can refuse to cry. Which he does.

Later, in the room she shares with her daughter, their mother

35

lies fully clothed on the double bed and sleeps, and it grows dark, and while George and Louise watch television in the gloom of the living-room, Earl writes:

Nov. 21, 1953

Dear Jack Bailey,

Maybe my first letter to you about why my mother should be queen for a day did not reach you or else I just didn't write it good enough for you to want her on your show. But I thought I would write again anyhow, if that's okay, and mention to you a few things that I left out of that first letter and also mention again some of the things in that letter, in case you did not get it at all for some reason (you know the Post Office). I also want to mention a few new developments that have made things even worse for my poor mother than they already were.

First, even though it's only a few days until Thanksgiving my father who left us last May, as you know, has not contacted us about the holidays or offered to help in any way. This makes us mad though we don't talk about it much since the little kids tend to cry about it a lot when they think about it, and me and my mother think it's best not to think about it. We don't even know how to write a letter to my father, though we know the name of the company that he works for up in Holderness (a town in New Hampshire pretty far from here) and his sisters could tell us his address if we asked, but we won't. A person has to have some pride, as my mother says. Which she has a lot of.

We will get through Thanksgiving all right because of St Joseph's Church, which is where we go sometimes and where I was confirmed and my brother George (age 10) took his first communion last year and where my sister Louise (age 6) goes to catechism class. St Joe's (as we call it) has turkeys and other kinds of food for people who can't afford to buy one so we'll do okay if my mother goes down there and says she can't afford to buy a turkey for her family on Thanksgiving. This brings me to the new developments.

My mother just got fired from her job as assistant bookkeeper at the tannery. It wasn't her fault or anything she did. They just fired her because she has these nervous spells sometimes when there's a lot of pressure on her, which is something that happens a lot these days because of my father and all and us kids and the rest of it. She got two weeks of pay but that's the only money we have until she gets another job. Tomorrow she plans to go downtown to all the stores and try to get a job as a saleslady now that Christmas is coming and the stores hire a lot of extras. But right now we don't have any money for anything like Thanksgiving turkey or pies, and we can't go down to Massachusetts to my mother's family, Aunt Dot's and Aunt Leona's and Uncle Jerry's house, like we used to because (as you know) the bank repossessed the car. And my father's sisters and all who used to have Thanksgiving with us, sometimes, have taken our father's side in this because of his lies about us and now they won't talk to us anymore.

I know that lots and lots of people are poor as us and many of them are sick too, or crippled from polio and other bad diseases. But I still think my mother should be Queen for a Day because of other things.

Because even though she's poor and got fired and has dizzy spells and sometimes blacks out, she's a proud woman. And even though my father walked off and left all his responsibilities behind, she stayed here with us. And in spite of all her troubles and worries, she really does take good care of his children. One look in her eyes and you know it.

Thank you very much for listening to me and considering my mother for the Queen for a Day television show.

Sincerely,
Earl Painter

The day before Thanksgiving their mother is hired to start work the day after Thanksgiving, in gift wrapping at Grover Cronin's on Moody Street, and consequently she does not feel ashamed for accepting a turkey and a bag of groceries from S

Joe's. 'Since I'm working, I don't think of it as charity. I think of it as a kind of loan,' she explains to Earl as they walk the four blocks to the church.

It's dark, though still late afternoon, and cold, almost cold enough to snow, Earl thinks, which makes him think of Christmas, which in turn makes him cringe and tremble inside and turn quickly back to now, to this very moment, to walking with his tiny, brittle-bodied mother down the quiet street, past houses like their own – triple-decker wood-frame tenements, each with a wide front porch like a bosom facing the narrow street below, lights on in kitchens in back, where mothers make boiled supper for kids cross-legged on the living-room floor watching *Kukla, Fran and Ollie*, while dads trudge up from the mills by the river or drive in from one of the plants on the Heights or maybe walk home from one of the stores downtown, the A&P, J. C. Penney's, Sears – the homes of ordinary families, people exactly like them. But with one crucial difference, for a piece is missing from the Painter family, a keystone, making all other families, in Earl's eyes, wholly different from his, and for an anxious moment he envies them. He wants to turn up a walkway to a strange house, step up to the door, open it and walk down the long, dark, sweet-smelling hallway to the kitchen in back, say hi and toss his coat over a chair and sit down for supper, have his father growl at him to hang his coat up and wash his hands first, have his mother ask about school today, how did hockey practice go, have his sister interrupt to show her broken dolly to their father, beg him to fix it, which he does at the table next to his son, waiting for supper to be put on the table, all of them relaxed, happy, relieved that tomorrow is a holiday, a day at home with the family, no work, no school, no hockey practice. Tomorrow, he and his father and his brother will go to the high school football game at noon and will be home by two to help set the table.

Earl's mother says, 'That job down at Grover Cronin's? It's only, it's a temporary job, you know.' She says it as if uttering a slightly shameful secret. 'After Christmas I get let go.'

Earl jams his hands deeper into his jacket pockets and draws his chin down inside his collar. 'Yeah, I figured.'

'And the money, well, the money's not much. It's almost nothing. I added it up, for a week and for a month, and it comes out to quite a lot less than what you and me figured out in that budget, for the rent and food and all. What we need. It's less than what we need. Never mind Christmas, even. Just regular.'

They stop a second at a curb, wait for a car to pass, then cross the street and turn right. Elm trees loom in black columns overhead; leafless branches spread out in high arcs and cast intricate shadows on the sidewalk below. Earl can hear footsteps click against the pavement, his own off-beat, long stride and her short, quick one combining in a stuttered rhythm. He says, 'You gotta take the job, though, doncha? I mean, there isn't anything else, is there? Not now, anyhow. Maybe soon, though, Ma, in a few days, maybe, if something at the store opens up in one of the other departments, dresses or something. Bookkeeping, maybe. You never know, Ma.'

'No, you're right. Things surprise you. Still . . .' She sighs, pushing a cloud of breath out in front of her. 'But I am glad for the turkey and the groceries. We'll have a nice Thanksgiving, anyhow,' she chirps.

'Yeah.'

They are silent for a few seconds, still walking, and then she says, 'I been talking to Father LaCoy, Earl. You know, about . . . about our problems. I been asking his advice. He's a nice man, not just a priest, you know, but a kind man too. He knows your father, he knew him years and years ago, when they were in high school together. He said he was a terrible drinker even then. And he said . . . other things, he said some things the other morning that I been thinking about.'

'What morning?'

'Day before yesterday. Early. When you were doing your papers. I felt I just had to talk to someone, I was all nervous and worried, and I needed to talk to someone here at St Joe's anyhow, 'cause I wanted to know about how to get the turkey and all, so I came over, and he was saying the early mass, so I stayed and talked with him a while afterwards. He's a nice priest, I like him. I always liked Father LaCoy.'

'Yeah. What'd he say?' Earl knows already what the priest said, and he pulls himself further down inside his jacket, where his insides seem to have hardened like an ingot, cold and dense, at the exact center of his body.

Up ahead, at the end of the block, is St Joseph's, a large, squat parish church with a short, broad steeple, built late in the last century of pale yellow stone cut from a quarry up on the Heights and hauled across the river in winter on sledges. 'Father LaCoy says that your father and me, we should try to get back together. That we should start over, so to speak.'

'And you think he's right,' Earl adds.

'Well, not exactly. Not just like that. I mean, he knows what happened. He knows all about your father and all, I told him, but he knew anyhow. I told him how it was, but he told me that it's not right for us to be going on like this, without a father and all. So he said, he told me, he'd like to arrange to have a meeting in his office at the church, a meeting between me and your father, so we could maybe talk some of our problems out. And make some compromises, he said.'

Earl is nearly a full head taller than his mother, but suddenly, for the first time since before his father left, he feels small, a child again, helpless, dependent, pulled this mysterious way or that by the obscure needs and desires of adults. 'Yeah, but how come . . . how come Father LaCoy thinks Daddy'll even listen? He doesn't *want* us!'

'I know, I know,' his mother murmurs. 'But what can I do? What else can I do?'

Earl has stopped walking and shouts at his mother, like a dog barking at the end of a leash: 'He can't even get in touch with Daddy! He doesn't even know where Daddy is!'

She stops and speaks in a steady voice. 'Yes, he can find him all right. I told him where Daddy was working and gave him the name of McGrath and Company and also Aunt Ellie's number too. So he can get in touch with him, if he wants to. He's a priest.'

'A priest can get in touch with him but his own wife and kids can't!'

His mother has pulled up now and looks at her son with a hardness in her face that he can't remember having seen before. She tells him, 'You don't understand. I know how hard it's been for you, Earl, all this year, from way back, even, with all the fighting, and then when your father went away. But you got to understand a little bit how it's been for me, too. I can't . . . I can't do this all alone like this.'

'Do you love Daddy?' he demands. '*Do* you? After. . . everything he's done? After hitting you like he did all those times, and the yelling and all, and the drinking, and then, then the worst, after leaving us like he did! Leaving us and running off with that *girl*friend or whatever of his! And not sending any money! Making you hafta go to work, with us kids coming home after school and nobody at home. Ma, he *left* us! Don't you know that? He *left* us!' Earl is weeping now. His skinny arms wrapped around his own chest, tears streaming over his cheeks, the boy stands straight-legged and stiff on the sidewalk in the golden glow of the streetlight, his wet face crossed with spidery shadows from the elm trees, and he shouts, 'I *hate* him! I hate him, and I never want him to come back again! If you let him come back, I swear it, I'm gonna run away! I'll leave!'

His mother says, 'Oh, no, Earl, you don't mean that,' and she reaches forward to hold him, but he backs fiercely away.

'No! I do mean it! If you let him back into our house, I'm leaving.'

'Earl. Where will you go? You're just a boy.'

'Ma, so help me, don't treat me like this. I can go lotsa places, don't worry. I can go to Boston, I can go to Florida, I can go to lotsa places. All I got to do is hitchhike. I'm not a little kid anymore,' he says, and he draws himself up and looks down at her.

'You *don't* hate your father.'

'Yes, Ma. Yes, I do. And you should hate him too. After all he did to you.'

They are silent for a moment, facing each other, looking into each other's pale blue eyes. He is her son, his face is her face, not his father's. Earl and his mother have the same sad, downward-turning eyes, like teardrops, the same full red mouth, the same clear voice, and now, at this moment, they share the same agony, a life-bleeding pain that can be staunched only with a lie, a denial.

She says, 'All right, then. I'll tell Father LaCoy. I'll tell him that I don't want to talk to your father, it's gone too far now. I'll tell him that I'm going to get a divorce.' She opens her arms, and her son steps into them. Above her head, his eyes jammed shut, he holds on to his tiny mother and sobs, as if he's learned that his father has died.

His mother says, 'I don't know when I'll get the divorce, Earl, but I'll do it. Things'll work out. They have to. Right?' she asks, as if asking a baby who can't understand her words.

He nods. 'Yeah . . . yeah, things'll work out,' he says.

They let go of one another and walk slowly on toward the church.

Dec. 12, 1953

Dear Jack Bailey,

Yes, it's me again and this is my third letter asking you to make my mother Adele Painter into queen for a day. Things are much worse now than last time I wrote to you. I had to quit the hockey team so I could take an extra paper route in the afternoons because my mother's job at Grover Cronin's is minimum wage and can't pay our bills. But that's okay, it's only junior high so it doesn't matter like if I was in high school as I will be next year. So I don't really mind.

My mother hasn't had any of her spells lately, but she's still really nervous and cries a lot and yells a lot at the kids over little things because she's so worried about money and everything. We had to get winter coats and boots this year used from the church, St Joe's, and my mom cried a lot about that. Now that Christmas is so close everything reminds her of how poor we are now, even her job which is wrapping gifts. She has to stand on her feet six days and three nights a week so her varicose veins are a lot worse than before, so when she comes home she usually has to go right to bed.

My brother George comes home now after school and takes care of Louise until I get through delivering papers and can come home and make supper for us, because my mother's usually at work then. We don't feel too sad because we've got each other and we all love each other but it is hard to feel happy a lot of the time, especially at Christmas.

My mother paid out over half of one week's pay as a down payment to get a lawyer to help her get a divorce from my father and get the court to make him pay her some child support, but the lawyer said it might take two months for any money to come and the divorce can't be done until next June. The lawyer also wrote a letter to my father to try and scare him into paying us some money but so far it hasn't worked. So it seems like she spent that money on the lawyer for nothing. Everything just seems to be getting worse. If my father came back the money problems would be over.

Well, I should close now. This being the third time I wrote to nominate my mother for Queen for a Day and so far not getting any answer, I guess it's safe to say you don't think her story is sad enough to let her go on your show. That's okay because there are hundreds of women in America whose stories are much sadder than my mom's and they deserve the chance to win some prizes on your show and be named queen for a day. But my mom deserves that chance too, just as much as that lady with the amputated legs I saw and the lady whose daughter had that rare blood disease and her husband died last year. My mom needs recognition just as much as those other ladies need what they need. That's why I keep writing to you like this. I think this will be my last letter though. I get the picture, as they say.

Sincerely,
Earl Painter

The Friday before Christmas, Earl, George, Louise, and their mother are sitting in the darkened living-room, George sprawled on the floor, the others on the sofa, all of them eating popcorn from a bowl held in Louise's lap and watching *The Jackie Gleason Show*, when the phone rings.

'You get it, George,' Earl says.

Reggie Van Gleason III swirls his cape and cane across the tiny screen in front of them, and the phone goes on ringing. 'Get it yourself,' says George. 'I always get it and it's never for me.'

'Answer the phone, Louise,' their mother says, and she suddenly laughs at one of Gleason's moves, a characteristic high-pitched peal that cuts off abruptly, half a cackle that causes her sons, as usual, to look at each other and roll their eyes in shared embarrassment. She's wearing her flannel bathrobe and slippers, smoking a cigarette, and drinking from a glass of beer poured from a quart bottle on the floor beside her.

Crossing in front of them, Louise cuts to the corner table by the window and picks up the phone. Her face, serious most of the time anyhow, suddenly goes dark, then brightens, wide-eyed. Earl watches her, and he knows who she is listening to. She nods, as if the person on the other end can see her, and then she says, 'Yes, yes,' but no one, except Earl, pays any attention to her.

After a moment, the child puts the receiver down gently and returns to the sofa. 'It's Daddy,' she announces. 'He says he wants to talk to the boys.'

'I don't want to talk to him,' George blurts, and stares straight ahead at the television.

Their mother blinks, opens and closes her mouth, looks from George to Louise to Earl and back to Louise again. 'It's Daddy?' she says. 'On the telephone?'

'Uh-huh. He says he wants to talk to the boys.'

Earl crosses his arms over his chest and shoves his body back into the sofa. Jackie Gleason dances delicately across the stage, a graceful fat man with a grin.

'Earl?' his mother asks, eyebrows raised.

'Nope.'

The woman stands up slowly and walks to the phone. Their mother speaks to their father; all three children watch carefully.

She says, 'Nelson?' and nods, listening, now and then opening her mouth to say something, closing it when she's interrupted. 'Yes, yes,' she says, and, 'yes, they're both here.' She listens again, then says, 'Yes, I know, but I should tell you, Nelson, the children . . . the boys, they feel funny about talking to you. Maybe . . . maybe you could write a letter first or something. It's sort of . . . hard for them. They feel very upset, you see, especially now, with the holidays and all. We're all very upset and worried. And with me losing my job and having to work down at Grover Cronin's and all. . . .' She nods, listens, her face expressionless. 'Well, Lord knows, that would be very nice. It would have been very nice a long time ago, but no matter. We surely need it, Nelson.' She listens again, longer this time, her face gaining energy and focus as she listens. 'Yes, yes, I know. Well, I'll see, I'll ask them again. Wait a minute,' she says, and puts her hand over the receiver and says, 'Earl, your father wants to talk to you. He really does.' She smiles wanly.

Earl squirms in his seat, crosses and uncrosses his legs, looks away from his mother to the wall opposite. 'I got nothin' to say to him.'

'Yes, but . . . I think he wants to say some things to you, though. Can't hurt to let him say them.'

Silently, the boy gets up from the couch and crosses the room to the phone. As she hands him the receiver, his mother smiles with a satisfaction that bewilders and instantly angers him.

'H'lo,' he says.

'H'lo, son. How're ya doin', boy?'

'Okay.'

'Attaboy. Been a while, eh?'

'Yeah. A while.'

'Well, I sure am sorry for that, you know, that it's been such a while and all, but I been going through some hard times myself. Got laid off, didn't work for most of the summer because of that damned strike. You read about that in the papers?'

'No.'

'How's the paper route?'

'Okay.'

45

'Hey, son, look, I know it's been tough for a while, believe me, I know. It's been tough for us all, for everyone. So I know whatcha been going through. No kidding. But it's gonna get better, things're gonna be better now. And I want to try and make it up to you guys a little, what you hadda go through this last six months or so. I want to make it up to you guys a little, you and Georgie and Louise. Your ma too. If you'll let me. Whaddaya say?'

'What?'

'Whaddaya say you let me try to make it up a little to you?'

'Sure. Why not? Try.'

'Hey, listen, Earl, that's quite a attitude you got there. We got to do something about that, eh? Some kind of attitude, son. I guess things've done a little changing around there since the old man left, eh? Eh?'

'Sure they have. What'd you expect? Everything'd stay the same?' Earl hears his voice rising and breaking into a yodel, and his eyes fill with tears.

'No, of course not. I understand, son. I understand. I know I've made some big mistakes this year, lately. Especially with you kids, in dealing with you kids. I didn't do it right, the leaving and all. It's hard, Earl, to do things like that right. I've learned a lot. But hey, listen, everybody deserves a second chance. Right? Right? Even your old man?'

'I guess so. Yeah.'

'Sure. Damn right,' he says, and then he adds that he'd like to come by tomorrow afternoon and see them, all of them, and leave off some Christmas presents. 'You guys got your tree yet?'

Earl can manage only a tiny, cracked voice: 'No, not yet.'

'Well, that's good, real good. 'Cause I already got one in the back of the truck, a eight-footer I cut this afternoon myself. There's lotsa trees out in the woods here in Holderness. Not many people and lotsa trees. Anyhow, I got me a eight-footer, Scotch pine. Them are the best. Whaddaya think?'

'Yeah. Sounds good.'

His father rattles on, while Earl feels his chest tighten into a knot, and tears spill over his cheeks. The man repeats several times that he's really sorry about the way he's handled things these last few months, but it's been hard for him, too, and it's hard for him even to say this, he's never been much of a talker, but he knows he's not been much of a father lately, either. That's all over now, though, over and done with, he assures Earl; it's all a part of the past. He's going to be a different man now, a new man. He's turned over a new leaf, he says. And Christmas seems like the perfect time for a new beginning, which is why he called them tonight and why he wants to come by tomorrow afternoon with presents and a tree and help set up and decorate the tree with them, just like in the old days. 'Would you go for that? How'd that be, son?'

'Daddy?'

'Yeah, sure, son. What?'

'Daddy, are you gonna try to get back together with Mom?' Earl looks straight at his mother as he says this, and though she pretends to be watching Jackie Gleason, she is listening to his every word, he knows. As is George, and probably even Louise.

'Am I gonna try to get back together with your mom, eh?'

'Yeah.'

'Well . . . that's a hard one, boy. You asked me a hard one.' He is silent for a few seconds, and Earl can hear him sipping from a glass and then taking a deep draw from his cigarette. 'I'll tell ya, boy. The truth is, she don't want me back. You oughta know that by now. I left because *she* wanted me to leave, son. I did some wrong things, sure, lots of 'em, but I did not want to leave you guys. No, right from the beginning, this thing's been your mom's show, not mine.'

'Daddy, that's a lie.'

'No, son. No. We fought a lot, your mom and me, like married people always do. But I didn't want to leave her and you kids. She told me to. And now, look at this – *she's* the one bringing these divorce charges and all, not me. You oughta see the things she's charging me with.'

'What about . . . what about her having to protect herself? You know what I mean. I don't want to go into any details, but you know what I mean. And what about your *girl*friend?' he sneers.

His father is silent for a moment. Then he says, 'You sure have got yourself an attitude since I been gone. Listen, kid, there's lots you don't know anything about, that nobody knows anything about, and there's lots more that you *shouldn't* know anything about. You might not believe this, Earl, but you're still a kid. You're a long ways from being a man. So don't go butting into where you're not wanted and getting into things between your mom and me that you can't understand anyhow. Just butt out. You hear me?'

'Yeah. I hear you.'

'Lemme speak to your brother.'

'He doesn't want to talk to you,' Earl says, and he looks away from George's face and down at his own feet.

'Put your mother on, Earl.'

'None of us wants to talk to you.'

'Earl!' his mother cries. 'Let me have the phone,' she says, and she rises from the couch, her hand reaching toward him.

Earl places the receiver in its cradle. Then he stands there, looking into his mother's blue eyes, and she looks into his.

She says, 'He won't call back.'

Earl says, 'I know.'

Kid in a Bin

Robert Carter

From opening till closing time, Anthony lives inside the wooden flip-top rubbish container which houses the plastic rubbish bags at McDonald's. His skin has become whiter and his brown hair is long and greasy; his eyes are cat-sharp. He is a bit over a metre tall which allows him to stand up straight inside the bin. In the mornings there is plenty of room for him to stretch, scratch, turn around or even curl up and doze. By mid afternoon the empty foam cartons of Big Macs and cheese-burgers and McFeasts swell the plastic bag and choke out the light and space, forcing him either to stand thin against the back wall or to lean into the rubbish, until one of the counter crew changes the bag.

At different times, Anthony touches his finger against the inside of the used chicken containers which are made from cardboard and have a small piece of tissue paper where salt sticks to the splotches of grease. Old men use the most salt, followed by boys, girls, older women and younger men. The least users are younger women – about the age of Miss Tomagin, Anthony's third-class teacher, last year. By licking the salt stuck to his finger, Anthony guesses the age and sex of the chicken-eaters. When the cartons come through the flip-top bin, he touches, tastes and guesses the owners before they reach the exit door. Anthony likes to watch the customers. For a really good look he waits for the flip-top lid to be pushed inwards by a depositor, otherwise he has to be content with one horizontal slit and two perpendicular ones about a centimetre wide surrounding the lid. Anthony's world comes in slices.

At 11.30 pm the night manager switches the air conditioning off, closes and locks the restaurant, and Anthony comes out to

49

make his dinner and prepare lunch for the next day. There is a mouse who lives in an empty Quarter-Pounder box alongside Anthony. They go in and come out, mostly at the same times. Anthony calls the mouse Nigel.

It is Sunday, 11.40 am. Outside the wind spits needles of rain. The customers are bursting through the doors, shaking like washed dogs, and laughing. Anthony is almost asleep in his bin – the air is humid and smells of sodden shoes and wet hair. Outside his bin is a boy exactly the same height as Anthony. The boy sees Anthony's eyes as he pushes his tray of rubbish through the swing-top. He pushes the flap again, and Anthony ducks down inside. He is too late, the boy sees his head disappearing behind the garbage. The boy pushes the flap once more and then reaches his arm in as far as he can in the direction of Anthony's disappearing head. His arm is too short to reach Anthony. The boy's mother sees what he is doing and shrieks at him to get his hand out of the filth. The boy goes to his mother.

'There's a kid in there.'

'Sit down, or I'll slap you.'

'There's a kid in the rubbish box, I saw his head.'

'Wait here, I'll get you another Coke.'

The boy waits for his mother to reach the counter and then goes back to the bin. 'Hey, you in there.' He tries to see inside by holding the flap open. 'What are you doing in there? You're not allowed in there.' A group of high school girls are giggling and nudging each other to have a look at the boy talking to the rubbish box. 'Why don't you come outside?' the boy says. The high school girls splutter into their thick shakes. The boy's mother returns with the drink, which she decides to give him in the car.

'It's probably a cardboard clown, or something,' she says.

'No it isn't, it's got real hair and real eyes, and it moves.' The boy's mother sees the high school girls looking at her and drags the boy out into the rain.

Inside the bin, Anthony eats one of the three Junior Burgers he prepared the night before. He watches the boy being dragged to the door, and the Coke being spilled as the boy looks and points back towards him. Anthony eats very slowly. Nigel is not in sight but Anthony pulls off a thumb-sized chunk of bun and places it in his box.

A newspaper comes through the flap and Anthony rescues it, saving it for later, when the shop is empty. Almost every day something to read comes into his bin. He has a small collection of torn-out newspaper items and one colour magazine article which has a picture of him, his mother and father and his sister. The newspaper ones have pictures of him alone. He carries them all in the pocket of his jeans, which are so tight that he has long since stopped doing up the top stud. The newspaper cuttings have begun to crack and split along the crease lines, from repeated opening and fiddling with greasy fingers. The magazine article is his favourite. Throughout stretching days in the dark bin, he feels the wad squeezed into his pocket, waiting for the eaters to go and the noise to stop. On wet nights the closing of the store takes longer. The floor is washed twice by the tired counter crew whose lips press together and whose name tags flop in time with the swing and pull of the mops.

Anthony listens for the sequence; air conditioner shut down, lights out, door lock click, and total quiet, except for the refrigerators humming downstairs. He waits several minutes in case the night manager has forgotten something and because he likes to anticipate the coming pleasure. He opens the hinged side panel of the bin from where the rubbish bags are removed and steps out into the customer area. The space rushes at him. Anthony closes his eyes for a few moments and then slowly opens them.

His legs and back are stiff and tight. He sits at a side booth made of blue plastic and watches Nigel run to the kitchen. It is still raining outside, he can see the drizzle sliding down the outer windows. With just the dull security lights on, he can see no further than the glass boundaries of the store. Once, earlier on, he attempted to look further by cupping his hands against the window and pressing his face against the pane, but all he could see was black, with some tiny lights too far off to matter, and some moths beating against the car-park lights.

He goes to the men's toilet, switches on the light and empties his bladder into the stainless steel urinal. He washes his face and moves it from side to side in front of the hot-air drier. Holding his hair back, he inspects his face reflected in the mirror. There is a tiny freckle-like spot on the bony bump of his nose which he feels gently with his fingers, screwing up his eyes for a closer evaluation. The remaining skin is the white of his mother's scone mixture before it was cut into circles with a tumbler and shoved into the oven. Anthony leaves the toilet and goes into the kitchen. From the under-counter refrigerator he takes two containers of orange juice. He switches on the hamburger griddle and the french fry vat and sits at the booth near the security light. From his pocket he pulls out the newspaper and magazine articles. He opens them carefully, bending the folds backwards and pressing them into flatness on the table top. With his fingernail he levers up the edge of the foil top sealing the orange juice and tears it away; some drops spill on the newspaper. He brushes them away with his sleeve and reads again under his photograph, with his finger sliding along beneath the words.

EIGHT-YEAR-OLD BOY STILL MISSING

The search continues for eight-year-old Anthony O'Neal who disappeared from his home on August 9th. A police task force has interviewed Anthony's school classmates, neighbours and relatives with no leads to the missing boy's whereabouts. Anthony's mother . . .

The griddle is hot and it is time to cook. Anthony stops reading and folds the articles back into his pocket. Outside he can hear the rain spatting at the glass, and the trucks changing gear in the distance. Nigel is running underneath the tables.

Anthony leans against the rubbish bag; he wants to go to the toilet and regrets drinking too much orange juice in the night. He concentrates on the customers through the slits. A tall lady with six children has come to have a birthday party. The children put on cardboard hats and make noises with balloons; one of them squeals every time the others take their attention from him – he is the birthday boy who shouts at his mother when he spills his thick shake across the table. His mother mops at it with table napkins and tells them he can have another one. He throws a piece of lettuce at the child opposite him who has turned his head away.

At the table alongside the birthday party sits a man and a girl. They are not talking, the girl has her back to Anthony and eats her chips one at a time and licks her fingers after each one. The man reads the *Saturday Morning Herald* and Anthony can see only the backs of his hands and the top of his head. As the man lowers his paper to talk to the girl, Anthony wets himself. It is his father, except that he looks older and his skin looks greyer. The girl is his sister, Meredith. Anthony feels for used paper napkins in the garbage. He finds some and attempts to blot up the urine before it leaks under the wooden bin and out into the customer area. Some of it escapes and sneaks across the floor and under the seat of the birthday boy.

Anthony presses his eye up against the horizontal slit. It is his father. Meredith appears to be bigger than he remembers. The floor crew supervisor discovers the leaking bin and dispatches a mopper to fix it. Anthony wriggles around to the other side of the bin to avoid detection when the side panel is opened. There is something he wishes to tell his father. A message he wants to pass to both of them. He takes an unused napkin from the bin and feels around until he locates a sundae container with some chocolate flavouring still in the bottom. He dips his forefinger into the container and prints his message in chocolate letters across the napkin. He folds the napkin delicately, careful not to smear the sauce all over the paper; he places it in an empty Big Mac box and watches through the crack. When everyone in the customer area is looking at something other than his bin, Anthony flicks the Big Mac box through the swinging flap and onto his father's table. Meredith jumps and showers chips over her father's paper.

'Someone threw a Big Mac at me,' she says.

'What?' Her father puts down his paper and collects the loose chips.

Someone threw this at me,' she says again, picking up the box and looking towards the birthday party group. She opens the box and takes out the napkin, unfolding it carefully. She wrinkles her face at the chocolate sauce.

'Throw it in the bin, Meredith,' he says.

'It says words, Daddy.'

'What do you mean?'

'The chocolate says words.'

'Let me see.' He reaches for the napkin. 'It does too.'

'What does it say?'

'It says, "STAY . . . OUT . . . OF . . . THE . . . something . . . STAY OUT OF THE . . . SUN." '

'What does that mean, Daddy?'

'I don't know.' The man's face looks puzzled. He stares at the birthday party group for a long time. There is no one else close enough to have thrown a box onto their table. He places the napkin and the box and the stray chips onto a tray and goes to Anthony's bin. He tilts the opening flap and tips the tray's contents in. Anthony has a close-up flash-view of his father's face. He sees the same ache as he sees in the men's toilet mirror. He watches his father and sister disappear through the exit door.

And the days and nights pass. Anthony's father and sister do not come into the restaurant again. Nigel becomes sick from eating rat poison and a lot of his hair falls out. Anthony drinks less orange juice and keeps checking his face in the toilet mirror. He cuts his hair with scissors from the manager's office. One night the manager comes back an hour after closing. Anthony is in the toilet. He switches the light off and hangs onto the clothes hook behind the door of the second toilet cubicle. The manager goes to his office. Anthony waits behind the door. There is a new message written on the back of the toilet door. He has not seen this one before; it says, 'Flush twice – the kitchen is a long way off.' Anthony does not understand the message. If the manager comes into the toilet, Anthony will lift his feet off the ground by holding onto the clothes hook. There is no sound coming from the manager's office. Anthony waits. He thinks of being inside his bin curled up against the fat of the plastic garbage bag, with the murmur of customers and FM music filtering through – impregnable. The fear of being discovered outside his shell is worse than nakedness – worse than peeling the rind of his sanctuary.

Anthony feels something brush against his ankle. In the darkness, his eyes search for movement. It is a large tom cat. The manager has brought his cat to hunt for Nigel. Anthony thinks that Nigel will die quickly this way. He kicks the cat in the stomach, anyway. It hisses and runs out of the toilet.

Within an hour the manager is gone. The restaurant is safe again and Anthony prepares his next day's lunch. He sees Nigel run into the kitchen and he smiles about the big cat. Waiting for the oil to heat, he spreads his collected articles on a table top – he smooths the magazine one, and looks at the picture of his family. He remembers when it was taken – on Meredith's fifth birthday, she got a bicycle with trainer wheels and it was in the background of the photograph. Anthony remembers giving her a large hazelnut chocolate which got left in the sun and which stuck to the foil and would only bend and stretch, rather than snap off in pieces.

Where the paper has been creased, some of the letters of the words have come away but this does not disturb Anthony; he has memorized most of them. He slides his finger under the words beneath the picture of his family. He reads aloud as he was taught in school, and sounds out the difficult words which, like many messages to Anthony, don't make much sense.

Missing schoolboy, Anthony O'Neal, pictured here with his parents and sister, Meredith, was last seen at his home on August 9th. Police believe his disappearance may be related to the death of his mother six weeks earlier. Mrs O'Neal died of metastatic melanoma, of which she was diagnosed six months previously. (Maliganant melanoma is a virulent form of skin cancer caused in most cases by exposure of skin to the sun.) A large number of reported sightings of Anthony have been

investigated by the police, with no success to date. Fears for
the boy's safety have increased as no indication of . . .
The griddle is hot and it is time to cook.

Anthony peers out through the horizontal slit in the bin. It is
cold outside and the faces of the seated customers go pink
around the cheekbones from the warm McDonald's air. The
rubbish comes in, tipped from its plastic trays. Anthony waits
with Nigel for the store to close.

No Longer the Warehouseman

James Kelman

What matters is that I can no longer take gainful employment. That she understands does not mean I am acting correctly. After all, one's family must eat and wear clothes, be kept warm in the winter, and they must also view television if they wish – like any other family. To enable all of this to come to pass I must earn money. Thirteen months have elapsed. This morning I had to begin a job of work in a warehouse as a warehouseman. My year on the labour exchange is up – was up. I am unsure at the moment. No more money was forthcoming unless I had applied for national assistance which I can do but dislike doing for various reasons.

I am worried. A worried father. I have two children, a wife, a stiff rent, the normal debts. To live I should be working but I cannot. This morning I began a new job. As a warehouseman. My wife will be sorry to hear I am no longer gainfully employed in the warehouse. My children are of tender years and will therefore be glad to see me once more about the house although I have only been gone since breakfast time and it is barely five o'clock in the afternoon so they will have scarcely have missed me. But my wife: this is a grave problem. One's wife is most understanding. This throws the responsibility on one's own shoulders however. When I mention the fact of my no longer being the warehouseman she will be sympathetic. There is nothing to justify to her. She will also take for granted that the little ones shall be provided for. Yet how do I accomplish this without the gainful employment. I do not know. I dislike applying to the social security office. On occasion one has in the past lost one's temper and deposited one's children on the counter and been obliged to shamefacedly return five minutes later in order to uplift them or accompany the officer to the station. I do not like the social security. Also, one has difficulty in living on the money they provide.

And I must I must. Or else find a new job of work. But after this morning one feels one . . . well, one feels there is something wrong with one.

I wore a clean shirt this morning lest it was expected. Normally I dislike wearing shirts unless I am going to a dinner dance etcetera with the wife. No one was wearing a shirt but myself and the foreman. I did not mind. But I took off my tie immediately and unbuttoned the top two buttons. They gave me a fawn dusk or dust perhaps coat, to put on – without pockets. I said to the foreman it seemed ridiculous to wear an overcoat without pockets. And also I smoke so require a place to keep cigarettes and the box of matches. My trouser pockets are useless. My waist is now larger than when these particular trousers were acquired. Anything bulky in their pockets will cause a certain discomfort.

One feels as though one is going daft. I should have gone straight to the social security in order to get money. Firstly I must sign on at the labour exchange and get a new card and then go to the social security office. I shall take my B1 and my rent book and stuff, and stay calm at all times. They shall make an appointment for me and I shall be there on time otherwise they will not see me. My nerves get frayed. My wife knows little about this. I tell her next to nothing but at other times tell her everything.

I do not feel like telling my wife I am no longer the warehouseman and that next Friday I shall not receive the sum of twenty five pounds we had been expecting. A small wage. I told the foreman the wage was particularly small. Possibly his eyes clouded. I was of course cool, polite. This is barely a living wage I told him. Wage. An odd word. But I admit to having been aware of all this when I left the labour exchange in order that I might commence employment there. Nobody diddled me. My mind was simply blank. My year was up. One year and six weeks. I could have stayed unemployed and been relatively content. But for the social security. I did not wish to risk losing my temper. Now I shall just have to control myself. Maybe send the wife instead. This might be the practical solution. And the clerks shall look more favourably upon one's wife. Perhaps increase one's rate of payment.

I found the job on my own. Through the Evening Times sits vac col. It was a queer experience using the timecard once more. Ding ding as it stamps the time. I was given a knife along with the overcoat. For snipping string.

I am at a loss. At my age and considering my parental responsibilities, for example the wife and two weans, I should be paid more than twenty five pounds. I told the foreman this. It is a start he replied. Start fuck all I answered. It is the future which worries me. How on earth do I pay the monthly rent of £34.30. My wife will be thinking to herself I should have kept the job till securing another. It would have been sensible. Yes. It would have been sensible. Right enough. I cannot recall the how of my acceptance of the job in the first instance. I actually wrote a letter in order to secure an interview. At the interview I was of course cool, polite. Explained that my wife had been ill this past thirteen months. I was most interested in the additional news, that of occasional promotional opportunities. Plus yearly increments and cost of living naturally. Word for word. One is out of touch on the labour exchange. I knew nothing of cost of living allowance. Without which I would have been earning twenty two sixty or thereabouts.

It is my fault. My wife is to be forgiven if she . . . what. She will not do anything.

There were five other warehousemen plus three warehouse-lads, a forklift driver, the foreman and myself. At teabreak we sat between racks. An older chap sat on the floor to stretch his legs. Surely there are chairs I said to the foreman. He looked at me in answer. Once a man had downed his tea I was handed the empty cup which had astonishing chips out of its rim. It was kind of him but I did not enjoy the refreshment. And I do not take sugar. But the tea cost nothing. When I receive my first wage I am to begin paying twenty five pence weekly. I should not have to pay for sugar. It does not matter now.

Time passes. My children age. My wife is in many ways younger than me. She will not say a word about all this. One is in deep trouble. One's bank account lacks money enough. I received a sum for this morning's work but it will shortly be spent. Tomorrow it is necessary I return to the labour exchange. No one will realize I have been gone. Next week should be better. If this day could be wiped from my life or at least go unrecorded I would be happy.

The warehousemen were discussing last night's television. I said good god. A funny smell. A bit musty. Soggy cardboard perhaps.

The boss, the boss – not the foreman – is called Mr Jackson. The foreman is called George. The boss, he . . . The trouble is I can no longer. Even while climbing the subway stairs; as I left the house; was eating my breakfast; rising from my bed; watching the television late last night: I expected it would prove difficult.

Mr Jackson, he is the boss. He also wears a shirt and tie. Eventually the express carriers had arrived and all of we warehousemen and warehouselads were to heave to and load up. It is imperative we do so before lunch said Mr Jackson. I have to leave I said to him. Well hurry back replied George. No, I mean I can no longer stay I explained. I am going home. And could I have my insurance cards and money for this morning's work. What cried Mr Jackson. George was blushing in front of Mr Jackson. Could I have my cards and money. It is imperative I go for a pint and home to see the wife.

I was soon paid off although unable to uplift my insurance cards there and then.

The problem is of course the future – financing the rearing of one's offspring etcetera.

White Places

Mary Flanagan

Celeste was first cousin to Cissy and Killer. Peachey was Celeste's Best, meaning her best friend. They always said 'Bests' to keep their true relationship a secret, and to be able to talk about the secret without hurting anyone else's feelings. That was the important thing, Celeste said, that no one know and that no one get their feelings hurt. Of course Cissy and Killer knew, but that was all right because they were first cousins to Celeste and so practically first cousins to Peachey.

The four of them had a club. The name and nature of this club was changed every three or four weeks, depending on what Celeste was reading. Celeste talked like a book and was fond of titles. She liked being President, Secretary, Madam Chairman and Grand Duchess Genevra Samantha Roberta della Rocca of Upper Vernocopium, a place even more important than Oz. The others let her be. But everyone knew it was Cissy who ruled.

Killer was the youngest and the fattest. Her shoes were always wet and untied with her socks sliding down into the heels. She had cold sores and was only in fourth grade. Her name was not really Killer. It was Charlotte Mundy Fletcher Doyle (mixed marriage: Roman Catholic and Presbyterian). Like just about every awful thing, the nickname was an invention of Cissy's. It came from one of their earliest games in which she and Celeste, starlets sharing an apartment in Beverly Hills, were stalked by a dangerous maniac known simply as The Killer. Their pretend boyfriends, a producer and his brother, the world's most daring stunt man, came over and over again to their rescue. Over and over they carried off Killer, bound and gagged, to a lunatic asylum. That was how it began – a crude game by later standards, but the name stuck. Cissy's and Celeste's parents tried, without success, to stop the children calling her by it.

'Chaaaaarrrrrrrrlotte,' Cissy would sneer across the dinner table, 'pass the potatoes, Chaaaaarrrrrrrrlotte.' Cissy wasn't afraid of anything. Eventually though, when she behaved like this, she would be sent off to bed where she would lie awake, waiting to pinch her sister's fingers with the nutcracker as soon as she fell asleep, which was usually within three minutes.

Mrs Doyle insisted the others be nice to Killer, share with her. Once she even had cried when her youngest daughter came home wet, though uncomplaining, from the swamp. They had been on a Royal Expedition up the Nile, led by Robert Redford and Cissy in a sedan chair. Killer had been thrown to the crocodiles after attempting to kidnap the baby Moses. Later, Killer had listened with her ear to the door as her mother reprimanded Cissy.

'Cissy, why are you so mean to Killer – ' She stopped impatiently. 'Oh for heaven's sake, you know I mean *Charlotte*.' It was too late. Mummy had said it and that made it true for ever.

Killer was six then, and Cissy was eight. By now the Pretends were much more complicated, and included a wide range of malice and glamour. (Cissy was maddeningly inventive.) But they were still variants on a single theme, and always ended with the Finding Out, the unmasking, at which everyone ran shrieking from Killer. Why the others like pretending to be weak and frightened and in danger when really they were so strong, stronger than she would ever be, Killer could not understand.

A tried and true Pretend, used when all else had ended in boredom or hair-pulling, was The Crazy Doctor. Killer, in disguise, would come to the grown-ups' bedroom – it had to begin in there – to prescribe for one of the three, who were always orphaned sisters. Eventually, they would guess her wicked intentions and race, screaming and laughing, to the attic, down again, through the upstairs rooms and out on to the lawn, pursued by Killer who was well-versed in the terrifying snorts and snarls she was required to make. Once outside, she would be caught, rolled up in a blanket, tied and taken off to be burnt at the stake, then released and made to play her part all over again until parents put a stop to the game.

They spent school vacations at each other's houses. Easter at the Doyles' and Christmas at Celeste's. This time, Peachey would be with them. Peachey was too small for her age, but very energetic. She was called Peachey because she once had been taught by her father to respond, at the top of her chipmunk voice to all enquiries after her condition with the answer 'Peachey Keeno!'

Celeste's father and mother were very indulgent. Even when the girls kept them awake until four in the morning, they did not complain very much. Killer always fell asleep first. The others ate crackers in bed and pushed the crumbs on to her side. They made raids to the kitchen for peanut butter sandwiches at two a.m. They came back and covered Killer's face with toothpaste. By the beam of a flashlight, they held a club meeting and read comic books under the covers. Peachey wrapped all their apple cores in paper and put the bundle down the toilet. The next morning the plumbing was blocked, and Killer stood, serious-eyed (she had been banished by the girls until three), watching Auntie Lillian mop up the bathroom on her hands and knees. She was given a jelly doughnut and allowed to watch Tom and Jerry until called to come and be a werewolf.

There was a blizzard. Killer was frightened by the silence and by the way the snow climbed the window panes. When she pressed her face against them, she imagined that she had gone blind, but that her blindness was white instead of black. It seemed hard to breathe, and she wondered if everyone were going to be buried alive. She thought she might like to go home. It would be nice to be tucked in by her mother and to watch her baby brother kicking his feet like a small fat bug or dribbling breakfast down his pyjamas. But she was too scared to tell Aunty Lillian any of these things. Besides, she had to stay here and be a Body Snatcher.

Celeste said that they should make puppets and a theatre and put on a puppet show. They thought of nothing else for the three days the blizzard lasted. Cissy and Celeste wrote a play and made posters to advertise the event, while Peachey and Killer worked happily and messily with balloons, cardboard tubes and papier mâché. Aunt Lillian was very patient. She and Uncle Raymond, along with all of Celeste's and Peachey's dolls, were forced to attend three performances, and to applaud, exclaim and congratulate on each occasion.

They experimented with the left-over flour and water paste, and invented, by the addition of sugar, milk, vanilla, corn syrup and a dash of laundry starch, a drink which they called Plush and which they forced Killer to taste after the addition of each new ingredient. That evening Killer threw up her supper. Cissy said that she thought it was disgusting, and that Killer was not mature enough to have been allowed to come.

When the storm ended, they put up signs and tried to sell Plush from a snow fort which they built at the end of the driveway. The snow was very high there, nearly six feet, because the blizzard had been such a long one and the snow-plough had had to come around so many times. No one bought the drink but Uncle Raymond who tasted it, tried to smile, and said he would finish the rest in the house, if that was all right with 'you girls'. They lost interest in Plush. It turned sour, stank and Auntie Lillian carefully asked permission to throw it out.

They decided to enlarge the snow fort. They built half a dozen each winter and knew everything about their construction. This was to be biggest they had ever made. To celebrate its completion, Cissy said, they must make up a brand new Pretend. Celeste agreed. Then Peachey and Killer agreed. They worked even harder on the snow fort than they had on the puppet show, talking and planning every minute for the Important Celebration Pretend. They were very excited, Killer could tell. She saw how much it thrilled them to make believe. To her, inside, it seemed almost frightening, the way they were always at it, never never getting tired of it. Why did they want to be something they weren't, to change everything into what it wasn't? Killer liked everything as it was – just plain with no Pretend, no titles, no talking like books, no ruling, no dressing up, no punishments, no Madam Chairman or Grand Duchesses or Cleopatras. But that was her secret. She knew that somehow it was wrong to like everything as it was, just plain. So she didn't dare tell them what she really liked.

What she liked was what they were doing now: sitting on top of their snow fort, watching people go by on the street – slipping and sliding, it was so funny – smelling the snow and sucking silently on the long icicles that hung from the maple trees and that tasted so sweet. Killer sat and sucked and felt happy to be with the others, happy about not having to do fractions, happy about the graham crackers and marshmallow they would be eating at four when Pretend was over.

Peachey, in a burst of Peachey energy, put snow down the back of her neck. Killer was soaked through anyway. They all were. But they hardly noticed, they were so warm with activity.

'Now this is the game,' Cissy announced, 'and you have to remember it. We've decided, so no changing the rules. Me and Celeste and Peachey are sisters and we're of noble birth. Our *real* mother dies and our father the Duke marries this woman Elvira, who pretends to be nice but who isn't – who's evil really. That's you Killer. You have to *seem* nice at first, remember that otherwise you'll spoil everything. Then we find out that Elvira has killed our *real* mother and is plotting to kill our father and steal our inheritance and make us homeless orphans. Then – this is Celeste's part, she invented it, she says I have to say so – a prince saves us! He catches Elvira making a cowardly escape. Then he marries Celeste and introduces me and Peachey to his two brothers who are Paul Newman and Steve McQueen. Elvira goes to prison. Do you hear that, Killer? Are you listening? You're going to be shut up in the snow fort – don't interrupt me, you *have* to be. Do you want to spoil the game for everyone else? That *would* be something you'd do. Anyway, my word is law, so you're going to prison. We'll come back for you after we've been to the palace to recover our gold and attend the banquet.'

'But – what about my graham crackers?' Killer knew she mustn't cry.

'You can have them later – if you do everything you're supposed to.'

'OK.'

Now they were carrying out the dolls to be the Duke's courtiers. Dolls and dolls – Celeste's dolls, Peachey's dolls, vacationing at Celeste's to visit their friends and relations. Killer didn't really like dolls, not even Dorothy, the most beautiful, with her long brown hair and bridal gown. She played with them, but they were not her friends. She preferred real things like babies and kittens and beach balls and toads and desserts.

Under Cissy's direction the Pretend went off perfectly. The arrival of the prince and his brothers was very exciting. With their invisible help, Elvira was tied and gagged and dragged off to prison. To make sure she would never again be free to plot against them, the three sisters and the three brothers placed pieces of cardboard (they had not told Killer this part) over the front and back entrances of the snow fort. These they covered with packed snow over which they dribbled a little boiling water. It froze almost immediately, making a nice smooth surface. Then they went off to the palace.

Of course they were not going to the palace. They were going to eat graham crackers with marshmallow and watch cartoons. They were going to tell Auntie Lil that Killer had run off to play with some children and didn't want her snack. They would be warm and giggling and eating her graham crackers. Afterwards they might take their sleds to McLin's field and have a snowball fight with the Dewhurst boys or go with them to the housing project and tip over the garbage cans.

Killer was cold and lonely. Her wet snow suit was no longer made warm by the heat of her body. They had tied her so tightly that she could not move. She looked round at her small prison of white. She could see, feel, hear the white, the whiteness of crazy nothing that scared her so much. She longed for Celeste and Cissy and Peachey. She wanted them to come and get her. She would play any game they liked, be any terrible person, she was so lonely here in the white.

They had walled her up with her accomplices in the plot – the three least loved of Celeste's dolls. They were no help. They had bad characters and did not care what became of her. Buster was a villain like she was – always trying to wreck plans, to spoil balls and ceremonies, to kidnap Dorothy. And June. June would do anything to attract men's attention. She was spiteful with short hair and told lies. She was also stupid and got the lowest marks at school. No one would ever marry June. Jackie, the dirty yellow and white rabbit, had been good at first when he arrived four years ago as an Easter Bunny. But he had allowed himself to be corrupted by Buster. Celeste said Jackie was a failure. His many crimes had made him unhappy, but it was too late for him to change his ways. Killer knew that she and Jackie and June and Buster were what Peachey's mother called Lost Souls.

Killer rubbed her tongue over her cold sore. It tasted like metal and tomatoes. She could never let it alone. Tomatoes made her think of last summer; picnics at Lake Acushnet, then fights in the car, after which she would cringe under the glare of Cissy's green eyes; Cissy and Peachey throwing jelly doughnuts at her and her throwing them back – the only time she had ever defended herself; Celeste covering her face with Ipana tooth-paste in the middle of the night; Cissy and Celeste frightening her with ghost stories and tales of torture so that she lay quaking in the dark as she was quaking now in the white; Quaker Meetings on the lawn ('Quaker Meeting has begun, no more laughing, no more fun, if you show your teeth or tongue, you will have to pay a forfeit'); the Mermaid game on the beach and Cissy whipping her with one of those long flat strips of seaweed. 'Peachey, you may take one giant step. Killer, you may take one baby step.' Oh the games, the endless games she could not resist. She must always play, never say no, never complain, please them by letting them hate her and be afraid of her. It was such a funny thing. Why was it like that? She couldn't really understand Pretend. And Pretend was so important. Pretend was everything, because without it you were only yourself.

How come Cissy and Celeste could make things up? They could think so fast. If she could think fast too, she almost realized before her thoughts slid back into simply people and things and events, she might not have to be always The Crazy Doctor. Not only could Cissy and Peachey and Celeste think faster and eat faster and run faster; they seemed to need less sleep, less food, less love than she did. They seemed, with the exception of jelly doughtnuts, not even to *want* any of those things. Killer longed for them. She longed for them now. But if she tried to get out of the snow fort before supper, they'd be sure to call her a spoilsport and to torment her all night long.

Better stay here a little longer and freeze. They would have to come back for her, because sooner or later they would need her for the games. They would not be able to have any of the good ones without her. She tried to feel very certain that they would come, but her heart was tightening, tightening and sinking. Her crime had been so terrible this time. No one could forgive her. Perhaps not even God could forgive her. She had broken the third commandment. She had killed the Duchess and tried to steal the inheritance. No, there was no chance of God forgiving her. He was going to let her freeze to death with Jackie and June and Buster, the Lost Souls. He would make the others forget her. He would make Auntie Lil and Uncle Raymond forget her, even her own mother and father probably. He *could* make everyone forget her. That kind of thing was easy for him. They probably had forgotten already. Or maybe it wasn't God at all. Maybe *they* wanted her to die, to freeze to death with Buster and June and Jackie. Get rid of the trouble-makers, the wicked ones, all at once. What about Mummy? She was always so kind, but that might be a Pretend too. She might really have been plotting with Cissy and the rest of them all along to wall up her little girl in a snow fort. Killer couldn't help it, she cried.

She cried until she had no more strength to cry. She began to give up, to fall asleep, to float away to a place where there was no more cold, where nothing was white, but all nice greens and reds and blues. Something was carrying her up to the sky, like Ragged Robin in the orange tree – up and up, away from the white. It was Uncle Raymond. He was pulling her out of the snow fort, he was untying her, he was picking her up in his arms, taking her to the house, muttering over her.

'Oh my God, poor Killer.' She could not open her eyes, she was so tired. 'My God, poor little Killer.' She liked Uncle Raymond. He was a nice man.

The hospital where Killer spent the next two weeks was very white. When she first awoke, she was frightened and thought that the snow fort had grown larger and cleaner and more occupied. It was warm in the hospital (she saw quite quickly that it *was* a hospital) and there were lots of people, mainly kind, who leaned over her, gave her things, asked her questions in quiet tones, took things away, moved her about – sometimes hurting her, though not meaning to – and gazed at her for long stretches of time through her plastic tent. Their expressions were of worry, sorrow or silly cheerfulness, if grown-ups, and of questioning uncomfortableness, if children.

Killer hardly spoke. She *could* speak, she knew that, but she did not want to. She looked back through her plastic tent at all those queer expressions. Sometimes she smiled at them a little. Mostly she slept. Slept and dreamt. She dreamed they played the Mermaid game, and that she chased Cissy and Celeste and Peachey for ever along an empty beach.

When she was very much better, they took the plastic tent away and let the children come near her. Cissy's green eyes were still defiant, but she spoke nicely to her sister and called her Charlotte. Killer understood that Cissy and Celeste had had some kind of punishment, but that now everyone was pretending that nothing had ever really happened.

Peachey held her hand and leaned over her. 'Bests,' Peachey whispered. Killer blinked at her. Did she mean it, was she making believe? Killer didn't understand, but smiled to let Peachey know that she was pretending she did.

Celeste even offered her Dorothy to keep for ever and be her very own. Dorothy with her bridal gown and long brown hair.

Killer hesitated. Then she spoke for the first time since the day in the snow fort.

'Can I have June instead?' she asked.

The Werewolf

Angela Carter

It is a northern country; they have cold weather, they have cold hearts.

Cold; tempest; wild beasts in the forest. It is a hard life. Their houses are built of logs, dark and smoky within. There will be a crude icon of the virgin behind a guttering candle, the leg of a pig hung up to cure, a string of drying mushrooms. A bed, a stool, a table. Harsh, brief, poor lives.

To these upland woodsmen, the Devil is as real as you or I. More so; they have not seen us nor even know that we exist, but the Devil they glimpse often in the graveyards, those bleak and touching townships of the dead where the graves are marked with portraits of the deceased in the naïf style and there are no flowers to put in front of them, no flowers grow there, so they put out small, votive offerings, little loaves, sometimes a cake that the bears come lumbering from the margins of the forest to snatch away. At midnight, especially on Walpurgisnacht, the Devil holds picnics in the graveyards and invites the witches; then they dig up fresh corpses, and eat them. Anyone will tell you that.

Wreaths of garlic on the doors keep out the vampires. A blue-eyed child born feet first on the night of St John's Eve will have second sight. When they discover a witch – some old woman whose cheeses ripen when her neighbours' do not, another old woman whose black cat, oh, sinister! *follows her about all the time*, they strip the crone, search for her marks, for the supernumerary nipple her familiar sucks. They soon find it. Then they stone her to death.

Winter and cold weather.

Go and visit grandmother, who has been sick. Take her the

oatcakes I've baked for her on the hearthstone and a little pot of butter.

The good child does as her mother bids – five miles' trudge through the forest; do not leave the path because of the bears, the wild boar, the starving wolves. Here, take your father's hunting knife; you know how to use it.

The child had a scabby coat of sheepskin to keep out the cold, she knew the forest too well to fear it but she must always be on her guard. When she heard that freezing howl of a wolf, she dropped her gifts, seized her knife and turned on the beast.

It was a huge one, with red eyes and running, grizzled chops; any but a mountaineer's child would have died of fright at the sight of it. It went for her throat, as wolves do, but she made a great swipe at it with her father's knife and slashed off its right forepaw.

The wolf let out a gulp, almost a sob, when it saw what had happened to it; wolves are less brave than they seem. It went lolloping off disconsolately between the trees as well as it could on three legs, leaving a trail of blood behind it. The child wiped the blade of her knife clean on her apron, wrapped up the wolf's paw in the cloth in which her mother had packed the oatcakes and went on towards her grandmother's house. Soon it came on to snow so thickly that the path and any footsteps, track or spoor that might have been upon it were obscured.

She found her grandmother was so sick she had taken to her bed and fallen into a fretful sleep, moaning and shaking so that the child guessed she had a fever. She felt the forehead, it burned. She shook out the cloth from her basket, to use it to make the old woman a cold compress, and the wolf's paw fell to the floor.

But it was no longer a wolf's paw. It was a hand, chopped off at the wrist, a hand toughened with work and freckled with old age. There was a wedding ring on the third finger and a wart on the index finger. By the wart, she knew it for her grandmother's hand.

She pulled back the sheet but the old woman woke up, at that, and began to struggle, squawking and shrieking like a thing

71

possessed. But the child was strong, and armed with her father's hunting knife; she managed to hold her grandmother down long enough to see the cause of her fever. There was a bloody stump where her right hand should have been, festering already.

The child crossed herself and cried out so loud the neighbours heard her and come rushing in. They knew the wart on the hand at once for a witch's nipple; they drove the old woman, in her shift as she was, out into the snow with sticks, beating her old carcass as far as the edge of the forest, and pelted her with stones until she fell down dead.

Now the child lived in her grandmother's house; she prospered.

A Tally of the Souls of Sheep

Keri Hulme

(NB: *Script*, *Notes, [Disinformation])

Location(s)

Kaitangata Bay is on the southern West Coast.

There, mussel-bearing rocks are swept by the boisterous Tasman, which is casual about snatching people with a swift white fist and bearing them off to the deeps. There, suitable low sandhills are covered with marramgrass and pingao and sand convolvulus. There, high cliffs and bluffs, and fascinatingly treacherous swamps, abound. And the bush can be impenetrable.

There, the Southern Alps rear in the near background. They are jagged fangs.

The car, to begin with – everything begins in the car – is travelling any scenic road. Choose your favourite route from any part of our thousand-mile stretch. Sooner or later, it will run into some sheep, grazing the long acre or moving from that paddock to this paddock.

The bach – we will come to the bach at Kaitangata Bay shortly.

*Kaitangata is actually in Central Otago. This is a dislocation. [Kaitangata means a dispute over eeling rights.]

*Ah, pretty nihinihi – perhaps a lingering CU on the shy pink flowers before shifting on to the winter-bronzed pingao. [He nui pohue toro ra raro.]

*battered 4–door family saloon, year and model immaterial.

*None of the characters refer to each other by name

*OED def. of *soul*: 'the essential fundamental or animating part, element, or feature, of something.'

*Any member of the ruminant genus Ovus.

Characters

The man is a freezing worker on holiday. He is middle-sized, solid, dark, and stolid (except for a nervous habit of chewing the nail of his left forefinger). His movements and actions are fluent, but aside from his eyelids (which flicker inappropriately) and his jaw muscles (which clench without, it seems, due reason) his face is frozen.

The woman is a housewife and mother, overtly devoted to kinder, kirche, kuche, and knitting. She is relatively tall, an ectomorph with a gaunt highly-mobile face. Her body is stiff and she believes it to be a rather messy casing for her soul. When she once unguardedly mentioned this to the man, he had a rare fit of hysterical laughter and was nearly sick into his sausages.

The daughter is just pre-pubertal, noisy, bossy, aggressive, and outgoing. She collects and pokes and explores.

The son is two years younger, a plump rather passive boy whose one passion is drawing. Anything on anywhere.

The main characters are accompanied by a cast of thousands.

Two passing shepherds and their pack of eye dogs and heading bitches.

An enigmatic pirate figure, one eye covered with a black patch, who seems to fish the beach at Kaitangata Bay.

Plenty of gulls and oyster catchers, tree-frogs, a morepork or two, and a cynical korimako.

And all these sheep.

Action

A bunch of keys swinging, one of them in the ignition.

The car interior, the four people.

The car radio –

'and in Wellington, Nelson and Marlborough, fine sunny weather. Overcast and mild in Buller, with showers expected later in the day. Rain on the West Coast and Fiordland increasing tonight, and in Southland, heavy rain and galeforce southwesterlies with mumble mumble mumble'

Woman (speaking over the weather forecast)· What's this place like anyway?

Man: Quiet.

Pan to passing fences, back to his face –

Man: O shit.

– long shot of the road ahead. There's a solid wall of sheep coming on. Two drovers behind the flock, one on a horse, the other on a farmbike, are pushing them hard. Several dogs weave round the sheep, which engulf the car, swirl and muddle round it. The dogs get noisier. The woman and kids stare in a bored fashion. The engine-sound pulses, competing with the barking and the bleating – the man is obviously revving the motor impatiently. A close-up of his face reveals his jaw muscles tightening. His eyes close quickly.

The long shot of moving sheep continues, but superimposed in the upper lefthand corner is a very swift montage of stills:

*sheep being flogged up the ramp to the sticking pens

Or, person displaying characteristics of the animal.

*A word about the sound track: it runs ahead of the action, sometimes. This happens in real life, too.

*Another word about the sound track: there is a phantom voice, which probably comes from the man's head because it is a masculine bass, but, gainsaying the character, it is rotund and flowery, an actor-poet practising his pieces.

[This montage will be used many times. It will even become slightly

scratched with use.
There is no accounting
for the realistic FX of
the playful mind.]

*a shiny steel hook hanging from a shiny steel band
*a stuck sheep and a smiling butcher by its side
*a shiny steel knife and a shiny sharpening steel across each other
*a sheep, eyes tightly shut, hanging head down
*a CU of a steel hook driven through a heel behind the tendon
*a knot of freezing workers in their surgical whites clustered together: no one is looking at the camera

The man's eyes open and his eyelids flutter. His jaw muscles unclench. The camera follows his gaze out the car window.
Some balky animals are close into the side of the vehicle.
Focus on one – on its loose lips and strange, empty, silvergold stare.
Sheep: Baaaaa.
Man (softly): Yeah.
Woman: Pardon?
Man: Nothing.

The sheep is shifted by a nipping dog. The last of the mob rattles past. A grinning dog runs after them. The drover on the bike is last away. He sticks one finger in the air in acknowledgement of their waiting, and roars off. He's grinning too.

*As he does, the
phantom voice intones
– *Phantom Voice*:
When the heels hang
from twelve o'clock,
the fingers just touch
six.

Action 2

The girl is tormenting her brother and he is whining for parental intervention. Outside, it is unremittingly scenic. The woman is knitting viciously.

Woman: Now what is this place like, *really?*

Man: Well Dave said. . . .

Woman: I don't know Dave. (She is frowning.)

Man: He's a nice enough bloke. Plays pool with the team sometimes. One of the admin lot though.

Woman: He's never been home.

Man: He's not that much of a mate.

Woman: Yet he lends you his bach for nothing and

Man: I mentioned at the end of the season I needed a damned good break – for christ's sake *shut up* –

(He doesn't yell, but says those five words very definitely. The children stop their squabbling immediately, though the girl pokes out her tongue, looking towards the backview mirror as she does. The woman compresses her lips hard, and inhales noisily.)

Man: a damned good break, so he offered it. Nice beach and good fishing he said. Sounded alright to me, particularly for nothing.

Woman: It wouldn't have cost *that* much to have gone to the camp as usual. The last five times have been so. . .

Man: Exactly.

Woman: *I* like the camp. (She is stabbing the needles through the wool.)

The man grunts.

Woman: It's got everything just like home. It's a change though. You know where you are.

The man grunts.

Woman: How much longer?

77

M   or   W?
W   [M]
WWWWWWWW
MMMMMMMM

The fanged equation

[Tally: to compare, for
the purpose of
verifying an account,
etcetera.]

*You will have noticed
many clichés already.
These small worn
truths are necessary.

Man: I don't know.

Woman: You don't *know*?

Man: Dave said when you get to the turnoff,
drive to the end of the unsealed road. He
didn't say how long the metal was going to
go on for. So we just keep going down this
road until the road runs out.

Woman: You do *know* which bach it is I
suppose?

Man: Dave says there's not too many of them
and his is the last one, right by the beach.
We've got the keys. And we can ask
someone.

Woman: *Dave* says . . . Dave *says*.

Silence. She stabs another stitch.

Location

*The bach at the beginning of the beach, Kaitang-
ata Bay*

It has four rooms – a small bedroom full of
double bed that the adults will sleep in; a tiny
bunkroom the children will share; a bath-
room-washroom-cum-loo, somewhere in
the background (it never figures as a location
but for the sake of verisimilitude . . .) and a
kitchen-living room, quite large, complete
with fireplace and two doors. The furniture
is dull, scarred, third-hand, dump-rescued.
There is a collection of paua shells on the
mantelpiece over the fireplace, ready to be
ashtrays.

Action 3

The man is fussing with a kerosene lamp.
The woman comes in, flings back the hood

of her parka scattering raindrops. She dumps an overflowing bag of groceries down.

Woman: O my g, . . . goodness.

Man: Neat isn't it? You wait until we get a fire going!

Girl: Mum, there's no electricity. There's no fridge or TV or phone or anything.

Boy: Mum, it's cold.

She pushes her hair away from her wet face with a tired gesture. Her face is full of lines.

Woman: O . . . goodness.

Man: Just as good as the camp eh?

He turns away so she cannot see his secret smile. The lamp is suddenly away in a flare of light and his face is full of odd shadows, odd highlights.

Action 4

A scene of peaceful domesticity. The man has built a fire and feeds it carefully, humming to himself as he does. The woman is arranging slices of kiwifruit on top of a large steak. She places another steak on top of the kiwifruit layer, making a macabre sandwich.

Woman (frowning slightly): We can probably use it all up before any goes off.

Man: What?

Woman: The meat.

Girl: What does that do? (She is watching her mother closely.)

Woman: Makes it tender. Makes it more tender. (She smiles slightly.)

The man frowns suddenly into the fire.

Man: Don't leave it too long. The last lot went like bloody jelly. No chew in it at all.

Woman (as though she hasn't heard): I wonder if we could use someone's freezer here. They surely wouldn't mind? (To her daughter.) Would you like to go and see who's home and maybe ask them that? There must be someone with the power on.

Girl: Can I have first pick of the steaks?

Woman: Go on with you. (She's smiling again.)

The girl takes this for 'Yes', and pulls on her parka, and stamps outside. The boy is drawing on the grocery bag. He takes no notice of anyone, and shields whatever he is drawing with his arm. Whenever the camera, handheld, edges closer to see what he is drawing, he swivels slightly, but not obviously, so the drawing is never quite seen. The man continues to hum and build up the fire, the woman to build her stack of green fruit and redly bleeding meat; the boy, to draw.

The door bursts open suddenly.

The girl has been running and her face is red as well as rainwet.

Girl: There's a dog up there and he's *starving!*

Man (standing abruptly): Where?

Girl: The last house on the hill. He's under the watertank and he's chained and he's *starving*.

Man: Did you try knocking on the door, see if anybody's home?

Girl: There's nobody home.

Woman: But where'd you look?

*The wood he uses is rata, freshly cut, obviously made ready for the incoming inhabitants of the bach. The resin runs out profusely, hissing and sparking in the flames. Tree blood.

Girl: Every place.

Woman: Nobody home? But that's silly. There's always somebody, people, somebody home. . . .

Swift cut to fawning dog, jaws grinning, tail in a flurry, ribs very visible.

His chain is fastened round his neck with a padlock.

His water dish is under the tankstand and thus, dry, despite the continuing rain.

He is slavishly grateful for the chops the girl feeds him, gulps them, pukes eventually, and, being a dog, eats everything again.

The man watches his daughter feeding the animal.

Man (to himself): Dave never said anything about a dog. . .

*Future generations will think the hardware we use on animals vicious, much as we view slave shackles and chastity belts now. 'Cattle prods? Snaffle bits? Dog whips and chains?' They'll shudder, stare horrified at electric fences and docking instruments, and denounce us as inhuman.

Action 5

The rain clatters against the windows.

The man and the woman are having a cup of Milo before going to bed. The fire has died down to a shimmer of coals and embers.

Woman: Are you *sure* there's no-one else here?

Man: Doesn't seem to be, just us. Good eh?

To her silence,

Man: Well, maybe they've all gone to a stocksale or a gala or something? Small country places are like this, everybody heads off together, right?

The woman hunches her shoulders and looks out the seagrimed windows into the night.

The rain keeps clattering at the windows.

Action 6

We are focused into the man's eyes. They stare. The eyelids flutter nervously. We draw out a little. He is listening intently.

The rain is still beating down, but the sound seems too heavy for rain. It is as though a thousand sheep are being driven at a fast trot outside the bedroom window, their sharp little hooves staccato.

Man: Rain. . .

The wind gusts, and the rain flock seems to move faster. There is a distant howling, a very distant clamour as though of miserable dogs.

Man: Wind. . .

Phantom Voice:
Do not draw your breath too deeply. Blood bubbles through the air.

[*Seems/As though*: prevarications.]

Action 7

Slow camera movement, pulling focus:
first, a tideline (quietly pan left)
then undulating sandunes, topped by pingao and marramgrass; darkgreen and bronze bush;
the blackly-ragged treetop line;
blue hazy hills, and finally,
the sharp cruel white peaks of the mountains.

Woman: Isn't it pretty!

Man: Yeah . . . bit toothy for comfort though.

The girl is yelling from further up the beach.

Girl: Look! Hey look what we found! Guts!

An excised liver, neatly tied up in a plastic bag.

The boy is dawdling behind his sister, doodling with a stick on the fresh sand page.

Man: Fishguts.

It's a pronouncement.

Man: Somebody's been catching a lot of something.

There are more innards, unbagged, along the shore.

In the distance, by the misty edge of a bluff, a thin wavering line of smoke arises.

Woman (heartily): Well, not *every*one's gone to town.

Action 8

They stand in an uneasy cluster round the fire. Most of the logs have burned to ashes, but the butts remain.

Man: Must've been burning for hours.

Woman (laughing uneasily): Those bits of sticks look like bones.

Girl: They *are* bones. They've got knobs each end.

Man: Some fisherman having a snack on the beach.

On the other side of the fire, away from the family, towards the bluff, a dozen severed dogfish heads lie in a neat row.

*Brief focus on the opaque gold eyes: tighten into the vertical slit pupils.

There are also a lot more guts, shining pinkly in the unexpected sun.

*Brief focus on the coiled wet lengths.

But the bones, calcined and grey and ashy, the bones are long.

Man: Pig bones.

He is frowning.

Man: Pig or something.

Action 9

It might be later that day. The woman and the children are walking back along the beach to the bach. The man is nowhere to be seen.

With all the wide freedom of the beach round them, the three still walk on one another's heels.

As they round the point into Kaitangata Bay, a person walks towards them.

Woman: Hello! Hey!

[Tally: (rare) short for tally-ho.]

The figure turns suddenly, as though a human cry affronted it.

Woman: Just a minute! Please!

It walks rapidly sideways, to the surf, but close enough for the three of them to see that it has one eye covered by a black eyepatch.

Woman: I beg your pardon, hello?

The figure turns deliberately on its heel, striding with haste into Kaitangata Bay. Into the roadway, presumably into one of the baches.

Woman (uneasily, to the children): He can't like company.

She smiles fixedly. The girl is unaccustomedly quiet. The boy is scratching some kind of ideogram upon a piece of seaweed.

Woman: Well at least we know there's really people back again.

Her eyebrows are puckered. She cannot understand how the figure disappeared so fast. A wave breaks close by.

Action 10

The woman is cooking, cooking chops. They are middle loin chops, and some of them have clearly once been ribs. The woman is cooking rib-bones and breast muscle.

A thin blue haze clouds the kitchen-living room.

A quick shot of a corner of the ceiling reveals many fly spots and a busy spider cocooning a victim and the odd swirl of cooked smoke.

The children trail in, strangely subdued.

Man: All this fresh air too much for you?

Girl: Don't like the flies ... and there's shadows round there.

Man: Round where?

Boy: By those cliffs.

Woman (sharply): What do you mean, shadows?

Boy (hesitant and whining the words) :
  Shadows ... just shadows.

  The man snorts.

Man: You'll be seeing bloody ghosts next – wash your hands for dinner.

Action 11

The camera will track the girl as she takes the gnawed chop bones up the hill to the dog under the water-tank stand.

She will call it cheerfully.

Girl: Nice food, dog! More nice food!

There will be silence.

The chain will be shown lying at full stretch, the padlock clipped onto the last link. There will be a line of dark pawprints leading away from the chain as though the dog had been worked hard and had gone on bleeding pads. The padprints will be visible because the dog has worn away all the grass.

It is bare and dusty ground under the tank stand.

Action 12

A door opens into the dark bunkroom.

The man stands black against the lamp-light behind him. The sound track is full of night sounds from the bush. The liquid trilling of tree-frogs. A morepork calling, and its distant mate answering. The querulous gutterals of a possum.

A camera peeps over the man's shoulder as he stares at his sleeping children.

They sprawl peacefully.

Because the room is full of bush-sound we can't hear them breathing.

[Tally: to count, or reckon up.]

Action 13

Very similar to Action 5 – focus on the man's staring eyes, pull out a little until we have him MCU: his arms are folded behind his head.

The bush sounds are very loud in this room too, but underneath them, on top of them, is the odd pattering rustle as of a large mob of sheep driven down a tarsealed road.

There are no noisy dogs, no miserable howling.

The sound of the sheep rushing past, just outside the room it seems, has overwhelmed all other sounds.

We widen the shot until we have the woman in view, and then tighten upon her.

She is lying on her side, back to the man, resting her head upon clasped hands.

We tighten the shot further to CU on her

*Fade down bush/fade up sheep.

Phantom voice (quite softly, just audible above the sheep-rustle):
When the hooter goes the killing stops. The quiet is eerie: no bleating just my mate

face. Her eyes are widely open. She is clearly
listening to something too.

Action 14

Very brief. The man is hunkered down,
head to one side, looking along the road that
ends by their bach.

There is not a sheep dropping in sight.

Action 15

The man is pulling mussels off sea-
guarded rocks. The surf smashes down and
spray flies over him. He yells. His face for
once is relaxed and triumphant and thor-
oughly happy.

He throws the mussels back to shore, and
the children scramble to get them before the
waves of the incoming tide do.

The woman is sitting on a high flat-topped
rock. Her feet are tucked under her. She
looks supple and at ease. She is knitting, her
ball of wool tucked away in a shoulder bag.
She shouts at the children, 'Be careful!' from
time to time.

Action 16

What happens next demands fluency in
camera action.

The family is coming back from the
mussel rocks, the children skittering ahead,
the woman striding with the man, the man
carrying the mussel-sack.

The camera is now airborne, sweeps out
over the sea in a wide circle, still centred on

caressing/the steel to
his knife 'See it shine?'
crooning through the
teabreak crooning to
that blade 'See it
shine?'

[How's your mind's
eye?]

87

the moving family group, to touch back on the beach behind them.

It moves up to the parents, swivelling round to the seaward side to contain them in profile LS, as they laugh and shout at each other, the man roused by the sea wildness and the woman aroused by the man in his wet shorts.

The camera then crabs round behind them again, as they stop for a swift hug. In the distance, we can see the girl race up to the bluff, the boy bend down and scribble something in the sand.

The camera pulls back. The children have raced round the bluff, the arm-in-arm couple are approaching it. They look very small, now, almost unable to be seen as people.

Action 17

Two lines of children's footprints, stark on the wet sand. They come to an abrupt stop, as though a straight-edged wave had erased them 3 seconds ago.

*Possible ending
Number One.

If we decide to go on:
the two adult faces, seen in CU, are blank, uncomprehending.

[*Action 18*]

The parents will check the sea, the cliffs, the beach, frantically. They will then assume the children are playing some macabre kind of hide & seek, and they will become angry.

They will then become tearful, hurl re-criminations at each other, at each self.

They will race back to the bach, arrive panting and dishevelled and exhausted.

They will look at each other in misery.

[Tally: to haul taut (specifically sails, fore or main loe).]

[*Action 19*]

While the woman marches determinedly up the hill to the baches there, the man leaps into the car. The engine keeps turning over, but won't catch. He checks the petrol – OK. The battery – OK. Everything seems to be connected properly. He is sweating and muttering to himself.

When the woman returns, slump-shouldered because there really is nobody anywhere here, except for themselves, the man points silently at the distributor cap.

Man: Somebody's taken out the rotor arm.

They look at one another, and then huddle together.

They press their faces into each other's shoulders and won't look up as the noise grows ever louder.

*A discontinuous soundtrack here, partly the man and woman's rushed breathing, partly the distant clamour of a pack of dogs intermingled with frenzied bleating.

*Possible ending *Number Two.*

[*Action 20*]

The man shakes himself, shakes free of the woman's deperate clutch.

Man: This isn't getting us anywhere. You check the beach again. I'll walk out.

He walks rapidly away. The woman calls after him.

Woman: But the nearest town might be miles and miles away!

He continues striding away into the distance.

Woman (quite softly): But what'll I do if I find them?

She turns wearily round to face the beach again.

A glint of light catches her eye. There is a camera on a tripod down towards the bluff and somebody hunched behind it.

She races towards it, yelling incoherently.

She is about 500 yards away, when the figure behind the tripod straightens – it is the enigmatic pirate person, and as the figure bends down again, it is apparent that it is looking through the viewer with the patch-covered eye. To its left, the landward side, stand two smaller people. They look almost the right size to be the children.

The woman stops dead. She peers ahead, her mouth dropping open. There is quite a seafog from the heavily-breaking incoming surf, but she can definitely see 3 figures. She sinks to her knees in the sand, covering her face with her hands.

*Seasound growing very loud as she does.

Woman: Dear God, I don't understand any of this, but thank you. Thank you.

She raises her head and opens her eyes.

*Possible ending *Number Three*.

There is no-one ahead of her, no-one by the bluff.

[*Action 21*]

The man comes striding round a bend in the metal road and stops abruptly.

The way ahead is blocked by a massive slip.

Man: Christ, no wonder there's nobody home. That must've come down in the rain just after we arrived.

*An impertinent korimako with

He steps cautiously onto the side of the slip. It is alright for his first hesitant dozen

90

steps, and then his foot slips on loose rock. He grabs at an uprooted manuka by his head. It pulls nearly free. The slope above and below him is starting to move.

A CU of his face shows a beading of sweat but his expression is curiously stolid. Unmoved.

excellent sense of timing begins to chuckle and chonk at this precise moment. Its call sounds over the ominous and increasing rumble of moving rock.

*Possible ending *Number Four*

[Action 22]

The man and the woman are sitting either side of the kitchen-living-room table. They hold steaming cups. They are hunched over them.

There is a grazed bruise down one side of the man's face, and one of his hands is bandaged. His lips are slack and his eyes are downcast.

The woman is trembling. She occasionally raises one shaking hand to her eyes, touching her lids.

The camera pans to reveal that both of the doors are blocked shut with chairs.

The camera pans once more, settles on the beachward window, focuses to where the bluff must loom in the darkness.

Two bonfires burn brightly there.

*There is the sound of vast flocks of sheep going by, the patter of hooves like heavy rain, the bleating frantic and hoarse. Hundreds of dogs yelp and bay. Both rackets are quickly drowned by a heavy shuddering beat, as though an enormous helicopter hovers directly overhead. [The man and the woman don't look out the roadward windows. They already have looked out, and the moonlit road is empty.]
*Possible ending *Number Five*

Finale

Kaitangata Bay in bright broad daylight is a pleasant busy sort of place. Outside one bach, a man is polishing his car. Next door to the bach at the end of the road (which is clearly unoccupied, with long grass surrounding it, and a general air of neglect) a sweetfaced white-haired lady is hanging out

[Tally: a stock or rod of wood, usually squared, marked on one side with traverse notches representing the number of sheep passed by the counter.]

washing. By the bach on the hillside, a young couple frolic with their excited dog.

Down on the beach, a solitary fisherman stands by a surf-rod. There is nothing tugging at the end of the cast-out line, and although the fisherman has but one eye, it gazes brightly, benevolently, on the wide spread of the Tasman sea, and he licks his lips.

The Drover's Wife

Murray Bail

There has perhaps been a mistake – but of no great importance – made in the denomination of this picture. The woman depicted is not 'The Drover's Wife'. She is my wife. We have not seen each other now . . . it must be getting on thirty years. This portrait was painted shortly after she left – and had joined him. Notice she has very conveniently hidden her wedding hand. It is a canvas 20 × 24 inches, signed l/r 'Russell Drysdale'.

I say 'shortly after' because she has our small suitcase – Drysdale has made it look like a shopping-bag – and she is wearing the sandshoes she normally wore to the beach. Besides, it is dated 1945.

It is Hazel all right.

How much can you tell by a face? That a woman has left a husband and two children? Here, I think the artist has fallen down (though how was he to know?). He has Hazel with a resigned helpless expression – as if it was all my fault. Or, as if she had been a country woman all her ruddy life.

Otherwise the likeness is fair enough.

Hazel was large-boned. Our last argument I remember concerned her weight. She weighed – I have the figures – 12 st 4 ozs. And she wasn't exactly tall. I see that she put it back on almost immediately. It doesn't take long. See her legs.

She had a small, pretty face, I'll give her that. I was always surprised by her eyes. How solemn they were. The painting shows that. Overall, a gentle face, one that other women liked. How long it must have lasted up in the drought conditions is anybody's guess.

A drover! Why a drover? It has come as a shock to me.

'I am just going round the corner,' she wrote, characteristically. It was a piece of butcher's paper left on the table.

Then, and this sounded odd at the time: 'Your tea's in the oven. Don't give Trev any carrots.'

Now that sounded as if she wouldn't be back, but after puzzling over it, I dismissed it.

And I think that is what hurt me most. No 'Dear' at the top, not even 'Gordon'. No 'love' at the bottom. Hazel left without so much as a goodbye. We could have talked it over.

Adelaide is a small town. People soon got to know. They . . . shied away. I was left alone to bring up Trevor and Kay. It took a long time – years – before, if asked, I could say: 'She vamoosed. I haven't got a clue to where.'

Fancy coming across her in a painting, one reproduced in colour at that. I suppose in a way that makes Hazel famous.

The picture gives little away though. It is the outback – but where exactly? South Australia? It could easily be Queensland, West Australia, the Northern Territory. We don't know. You could never find that spot.

He is bending over (feeding?) the horse, so it is around dusk. This is borne out by the length of Hazel's shadow. It is probably in the region of 5 p.m. Probably still over the hundred mark. What a place to spend the night. The silence would have already begun.

Hazel looks unhappy. I can see she is having second thoughts. All right, it was soon after she had left me; but she is standing away, in the foreground, as though they're not speaking. See that? Distance = doubts. They've had an argument.

Of course, I want to know all about him. I don't even know his name. In Drysdale's picture he is a silhouette. A completely black figure. He could have been an Aborigine; by the late forties I understand some were employed as drovers.

But I rejected that.

I took a magnifying glass. I wanted to see the expression on his face. What colour is his hair? Magnified, he is nothing but brush strokes. A real mystery man.

It is my opinion, however, that he is a small character. See his size in relation to the horse, to the wheels of the cart. Either that, or it is a ruddy big horse.

It begins to fall into place.

I had an argument with our youngest, Kay, the other day. Both she and Trevor sometimes visit me, I might add, she hasn't married and has her mother's general build. She was blaming me, said people said mum was a good sort.

Right. I nodded.

'Then why did she scoot?'

'Your mother,' I said thinking quickly, 'had a silly streak.'

If looks could kill!

I searched around – 'She liked to paddle in water!'

Kay gave a nasty laugh, 'What? You're the limit. You really are.'

Of course, I hadn't explained properly. And I didn't even know then she had gone off with a drover.

Hazel was basically shy, even with me: quiet, generally non-committal. At the same time, I can imagine her allowing herself to be painted so soon after running off without leaving even a phone number or forwarding address. It fits. It sounds funny, but it does.

This silly streak. Heavy snow covered Mt Barker for the first time and we took the Austin up on the Sunday. From a visual point of view it was certainly remarkable. Our gum trees and stringy barks somehow do not go with the white stuff, not even the old Ghost Gum. I mentioned this to Hazel but she just ran into it and began chucking snowballs at me. People were laughing. Then she fell in up to her knees, squawking like a schoolgirl. I didn't mean to speak harshly, but I went up to her, 'Come on, don't be stupid. Get up.' She went very quiet. She didn't speak for hours.

Kay of course wouldn't remember that.

With the benefit of hindsight, and looking at this portrait by Drysdale, I can see Hazel had a soft side. I think I let her clumsiness get me down. The sight of sweat patches under her arms, for example, somehow put me in a bad mood. It irritated me the way she chopped wood. I think she enjoyed chopping wood. There was the time I caught her lugging into the house the ice for the ice chest – this is just after the war. The ice man didn't seem to notice; he was following, working out his change. It somehow made her less attractive in my eyes, I don't know why. And then of course she killed that snake down at the beach shack we took one Christmas. I happened to lift the lid of the incinerator – a black brute, its head bashed in. 'It was under the house,' she explained.

It was a two-roomed shack, bare floorboards. It had a primus stove, and an asbestos toilet down the back. Hazel didn't mind. Quite the contrary; when it came time to leave she was downcast. I had to be at town for work.

The picture reminds me. It was around then Hazel took to wearing just a slip around the house. And bare feet. The dress in the picture looks like a slip. She even used to burn rubbish in it down the back.

I don't know.

'Hello, missus!' I used to say, entering the kitchen. Not perfect perhaps, especially by today's standards, but that is my way of showing affection. I think Hazel understood. Sometimes I could see she was touched.

I mention that to illustrate our marriage was not all nit-picking and argument. When I realized she had gone I sat for nights in the lounge with the lights out. I am a dentist. You can't have shaking hands and be a dentist. The word passed around. Only now, touch wood, has the practice picked up to any extent.

Does this explain at all why she left?

Not really.

To return to the picture. Drysdale has left out the flies. No doubt he didn't want Hazel waving her hand, or them crawling over her face. Nevertheless, this is a serious omission. It is altering the truth for the sake of a pretty picture, or 'composition'. I've been up around there – and there are hundreds of flies. Not necessarily germ carriers, 'bush flies' I think these are called; and they drive you mad. Hazel of course accepted everything without a song and dance. She didn't mind the heat, or the flies.

It was a camping holiday. We had one of those striped beach tents shaped like a bell. I thought at the time it would prove handy – visible from the air – if we got lost. Now that is a point. Although I will never forget the colours and the assortment of rocks I saw up there I have no desire to return, none. I realized one night. Standing a few yards from the tent, the cavernous sky and the silence all round suddenly made me shudder. I felt lost. It defied logic. And during the day the bush, which is small and prickly, offered no help (I was going to say 'sympathy'). It was stinking hot.

Yet Hazel was in her element, so much so she seemed to take no interest in the surroundings. She acted as if she were part of it. I felt ourselves moving apart, as if I didn't belong there, especially with her. I felt left out. My mistake was to believe it was a passing phase, almost a form of indulence on her part.

An unfortunate incident didn't help. We were looking for a camp site. 'Not yet. No, not there,' I kept saying – mainly to myself, for Hazel let me go on, barely saying a word. At last I found a spot. A tree showed in the dark. We bedded down. Past midnight we were woken by a terrifying noise and lights. The children all began to cry. I had pitched camp alongside the Adelaide – Port Augusta railway line.

Twenty or thirty miles north of Port Augusta I turned back. I had to. We seemed to be losing our senses. We actually met a drover somewhere around there. He was off on the side making tea. When I asked where were his sheep, or the cattle, he gave a wave of his hand. For some reason this amused Hazel. She squatted down. I can still see her expression, silly girl.

The man didn't say much. He did offer tea though. 'Come on,' said Hazel, smiling up at me.

Hazel and her silly streak – she knew I wanted to get back. The drover, a diplomat, poked at the fire with a stick.

I said: 'You can if you want. I'll be in the car.'

That is all.

I recall the drover as a thin head in a khaki hat, not talkative, with dusty boots. He is indistinct. Is it him? I don't know. Hazel – it is Hazel and the rotten landscape that dominate everything.

Tree

Neil Jordan

There were two things he could not do, one was drive a car, the other was step out of a car. So she was driving when she saw the tree, she had been driving all week. He was telling her another point of interest about the crumbling landscape round them, the landscape with more points of historical interest per square mile than – something about a woman who was to have a baby at midnight, but who sat on a rock and kept the baby back till dawn, an auspicious hour, and the rock ever after had a dent in it and was called Brigid's –

She saw the tree from about a mile off, since the road they were driving was very straight, rising slowly all the time, with low slate walls that allowed a perfect, rising view. It was late summer and the tree looked like a whitethorn tree and she forgot about local history and remembered suddenly and clearly holidays she had taken as a child, the old Ford Coupe driving down the country lanes and the flowering whitethorn dotting the hedges. It would appear in regular bursts, between yards of dull green. It would be a rich, surprised cream colour, it would remind her of a fist opened suddenly, the fingers splayed heavenwards. It would delight her unutterably and her head would jerk forwards and backwards as each whitethorn passed.

Then something struck her and she stopped the car suddenly. She jerked forward and she heard his head striking the windscreen.

'What's–' he began, then he felt his head. She had interrupted him.

'I'm sorry,' she said, 'but look at that tree.'

'There are no trees.' His fingers had searched his forehead and found a bump. He would be annoyed. 'This is a limestone landscape.'

She pointed with her finger. His eyes followed her finger and the edges of his eyelids creased as he stared.

'Well there is a tree, then.'

'It's a whitethorn tree,' she said. 'It's flowering.'

'That's impossible,' he said. She agreed.

The thought that it was impossible made her warm, with a childish warm delight. She felt the muscles in her legs glow, stiff from the accelerator. The impossible possible she thought. She knew the phrase meant nothing. She remembered an opera where a walking-stick grew flowers. She thought of death, which makes anything possible. She looked at his long teutonic face, such perfection of feature that it seemed a little deformed.

'But it's white, isn't it?'

'Then,' he said, 'it couldn't be a whitethorn.'

'But it's white.'

'It's the end of August.'

She turned the key in the ignition and drove again. She thought of his slight, perfect body beside her in bed, of its recurrent attraction for her. She thought of his hatred of loud sounds, his habit of standing in the background, the shadows, yet seeming to come forward. She thought of how his weaknesses became his strengths, with a cunning that was perhaps native to his weakness. She thought of all the times they had talked it out, every conceivable mutation in their relation-ship, able and disable, every possible emotional variant, con-tempt to fear, since it's only by talking of such things that they are rendered harmless. She drove the car slowly, on the slight upward hill, the several yards to the pub they had arranged to stop at.

'It is possible.'

'What is?'

'Everything's possible.'

He asked would they go in then.

She opened her door and walked around the car and opened his door. She waited till he had lifted his good leg clear of the car, then held his arm while he balanced himself and lifted out the stiff leg.

She watched him walk across the road and marvelled again at how the stiffness gave him, if anything, a kind of brittle elegance. She saw him reach the pub door, go inside without looking back. Then she looked up the road, curving upwards and the tree off from the road, in the distance. It was still white. Unutterably white.

The pub was black after the light outside. He was sitting by the long bar, drinking a glass of beer. Beside him was another glass, and a bottle of tonic-water. Behind the bar was a woman with a dark western face, ruined by a pair of steel glasses. She was talking, obviously in answer to a question of his.

'Cornelius O'Brien lived in the lower one,' she said. 'Owned more than them all put together. A great packer.'

'Packer?'

'Jury-packer,' she said, as if it was a term of office.

He leant forward, his face eager with another question. She slipped into the seat beside him. She poured the tonic-water into the glass, wondering why it was he always bought her that. She must have expressed a preference for it once, but she couldn't remember when. Once she drank whiskey, she remembered, and now she drank tonic. And sometime in between she had changed.

'Why did you get me this,' she interrupted.

He looked up surprised. Then smiled, a fluid smile.

'Because you always drink it.'

'Once I drank whiskey.'

The wrinkles formed in clusters round his eyes.

'I remember. Yes, Why did you stop?'

She drank it quietly, trying to remember, listening to his further question about the crumbling castles. The woman answered, speaking the way children do, using words they don't understand. She used phrases to describe the dead inhabitants of those castles that were like litanies, that had filtered through years to her, that must have once had meaning. She was cleaning a glass and her eyes looked vacant as her mouth spoke the forgotten phrases.

She stared at the ice in her tonic water. She watched it melt, slowly. She wondered about phrases, how they either retain the ghost of a meaning they once had, or grope towards a meaning they might have. Then she suddenly, vitally, remembered the taste of whiskey. Gold, and volatile, filling not the tongue but the whole mouth.

'Whitethorn,' she said, loud, out of the blue, as if it were a statement.

The woman stopped cleaning the glass and looked at her. He put his hand round his glass and looked at her.

'Have you come far, then?' the woman asked.

'A long way alright.' the woman said. Then she glanced from him to her.

'Is it herself who drives?'

She saw his hand tighten round the glass. She remembered the taste of whiskey. She said:

'He has a bad leg. There are two things he can't do. Get out of a car, and drive a car. But otherwise everything's fine. Isn't that right John?'

He had already gone towards the door. She fumbled in her pocket to find fifty pence. She couldn't and so she left a pound.

He was standing by the door of the car.

'Why did you have to jabber on like that?'

'Why did you order me a tonic?'

'You're impossible.'

'Nothing's impossible.'

'Get in.'

She drove. He swore at her in considered, obscene phrases as she drove. She knew he would swear like that, slowly and sadistically, scraping every crevice of her womanhood, till his anger had died down. So she drove with her eyes on the blaze far up the road, like a surprised fist with its fingers towards the sky, the brilliant cream-white of a dice-cube. As she drove nearer it seemed to swim in front of her eyes, to expand, to explode, and yet still retain its compact white. She could hear their breathing as she drove, hers fast like an animal that is running, his slow, like an animal that must stand in the one place. Then the white seemed to fill her vision and she stopped. She looked at the trunk below the white and the long field between it and the road. Then she looked at him.

He was crying, and his face looked more beautiful than ever through the tears.

'I love you,' he said.

'I'm leaving,' she said.

'Again?' he asked.

He grabbed her, half angry, half afraid, but she had the door open already and she slipped away. She walked round the car and looked at him.

'I don't – ' she began, but her words were drowned by the sudden blast of the horn. His hand was on it, his knuckles white, his body was bent forward as if all his strength was needed to keep the horn pressed. She could hear the awful blare in her ears and could see his lips moving, saying something. She shouted at him to take his hand off and his lips moved again, saying the same something, the same three words. She made out the three words then and turned from his face and ran.

She ran to the slate wall and clambered over it, scraping her shins. She felt the grass under her feet and put her hands over her ears. She was shocked by the sudden silence, like a sudden immersion in water. She was walking, but it was as if through a mental landscape, no sound but the strange humming of her eardrums. She felt she had closed her eyes and found this field, not driven to it. She knew her feet were walking her towards the tree, but it was as if the tree was coming towards her. The landscape rising with each step and each step bringing the landscape nearer. The tree on the hill, with its white made manageable now, small, tangible, familiar. She counted her steps like a little girl does and each step misplaced her hands and rang in her ears. Then something struck her about the tree, not really white, more an off-grey colour. She took three more steps and it came nearer, with the hill behind it, and its blossoms seemed to flap. But blossoms don't flap, she thought, they are still and pristine, they burst or moult, not flap and she must have run then for it came nearer in several large leaps.

And it was there then, bare rough whitethorn with scores of

tiny rags tied to each branch, pieces of handkerchief, shirt-tails, underwear, shift, masquerading as blossom. She thought of people wishing, tying these proxy blossoms. She thought of her and her hope that it had blossomed and them, making it blossom with their hope. She wondered again what hope meant, what impossible meant, but there was less scope to her wondering. She saw faded holy pictures nailed to the bottom of the trunk but couldn't read the pleas written on them. She took her hands from her ears to tear one off and the wail of the horn flooded her again, distant, plaintive, pleading. She tore a picture off, parts of it crumbled in her fingers, but she read 'To Brigid for favours granted, August 1949.' And the horn wailed like pain.

Significant Moments in the Life of My Mother

Margaret Atwood

When my mother was very small, someone gave her a basket of baby chicks for Easter. They all died.

'I didn't know you weren't supposed to pick them up,' says my mother. 'Poor little things. I laid them out in a row on a board, with their little legs sticking out straight as pokers, and wept over them. I'd loved them to death.'

Possibly this story is meant by my mother to illustrate her own stupidity, and also her sentimentality. We are to understand she wouldn't do such a thing now.

Possibly it's a commentary on the nature of love; though, knowing my mother, this is unlikely.

My mother's father was a country doctor. In the days before cars he drove a team of horses and a buggy around his territory, and in the days before snow ploughs he drove a team and a sleigh, through blizzards and rainstorms and in the middle of the night, to arrive at houses lit with oil lamps where water would be boiling on the wood range and flannel sheets warming on the plate rack, to deliver babies who would subsequently be named after him. His office was in the house, and as a child my mother would witness people arriving at the office door, which was reached through the front porch, clutching parts of themselves – thumbs, fingers, toes, ears, noses – which had accidentally been cut off, pressing these severed parts to the raw stumps of their bodies as if they could be stuck there like dough, in the mostly vain hope that my grandfather would be able to sew them back on, heal the gashes made in them by axes, saws, knives, and fate.

My mother and her younger sister would loiter near the closed office door until shooed away. From behind it would come groans, muffled screams, cries for help. For my mother, hospitals have never been glamorous places, and illness offers no respite or holiday. 'Never get sick,' she says, and means it. She hardly ever does.

Once, though, she almost died. It was when her appendix burst. My grandfather had to do the operation. He said later that he shouldn't have been the person to do it: his hands were shaking too much. This is one of the few admissions of weakness on his part that my mother has ever reported. Mostly he is portrayed as severe and in charge of things. 'We all respected him, though,' she says. 'He was widely respected.' (This is a word which has slipped a little in the scale since my mother's youth. It used to outrank *love*.)

It was someone else who told me the story of my grandfather's muskrat farm: how he and one of my mother's uncles fenced in the swamp at the back of their property and invested my mother's maiden aunt's savings in muskrats. The idea was that these muskrats would multiply and eventually be made into muskrat coats, but an adjoining apple farmer washed his spraying equipment upstream, and the muskrats were all killed by the poison, as dead as doornails. This was during the Depression, and it was no joke.

When they were young – this can cover almost anything these days, but I put it at seven or eight – my mother and her sister had a tree house, where they spent some of their time playing dolls' tea parties and so forth. One day they found a box of sweet little bottles outside my grandfather's dispensary. The bottles were being thrown out, and my mother (who has always hated waste) appropriated them for use in their dolls' house. The bottles were full of yellow liquid, which they left in because it looked so pretty. It turned out that these were urine samples.

'We got Hail Columbia for that,' says my mother. 'But what did we know?'

My mother's family lived in a large white house near an apple orchard, in Nova Scotia. There was a barn and a carriage-house; in the kitchen there was a pantry. My mother can remember the days before commercial bakeries, when flour came in barrels and all the bread was made at home. She can remember the first radio broadcast she ever heard, which was a singing commercial about socks.

In this house there were many rooms. Although I have been there, although I have seen the house with my own eyes, I still don't know how many. Parts of it were closed off, or so it seemed; there were back staircases. Passages led elsewhere. Five children lived in it, two parents, a hired man and a hired girl, whose names and faces kept changing. The structure of the house was hierarchical, with my grandfather at the top, but its secret life – the life of pie crusts, clean sheets, the box of rags in the linen closet, the loaves in the oven – was female. The house, and all the objects in it, crackled with static electricity; undertows washed through it, the air was heavy with things that were known but not spoken. Like a hollow log, a drum, a church, it amplified, so that conversations whispered in it sixty years ago can be half-heard even today.

In this house you had to stay at the table until you had eaten everything on your plate. ' "Think of the starving Armenians," mother used to say,' says my mother. 'I didn't see how eating my bread crusts was going to help them out one jot.'

It was in this house that I first saw a stalk of oats in a vase, each oat wrapped in the precious silver paper which had been carefully saved from a chocolate box. I thought it was the most wonderful thing I had ever seen, and began saving silver paper myself. But I never got around to wrapping the oats, and in any case I didn't know how. Like many other art forms of vanished civilizations, the techniques for this one have been lost and cannot quite be duplicated.

'We had oranges at Christmas,' says my mother. 'They came all the way from Florida; they were very expensive. That was the big treat: to find an orange in the toe of your stocking. It's funny to remember how good they tasted, now.'

When she was sixteen, my mother had hair so long she could sit on it. Women were bobbing their hair by then; it was getting to be the twenties. My mother's hair was giving her headaches, she says, but my grandfather, who was very strict, forbade her to cut it. She waited until one Saturday when she knew he had an appointment with the dentist.

'In those days there was no freezing,' says my mother. 'The drill was worked with a foot pedal, and it went *grind, grind, grind*. The dentist himself had brown teeth: he chewed tobacco, and he would spit the tobacco juice into a spittoon while he was working on your teeth.'

Here my mother, who is a good mimic, imitates the sounds of the drill and the tobacco juice: '*Rrrrr! Rrrrr! Rrrrr! Phtt! Rrrrr!* '*Rrrrr! Rrrrr! Phtt!* It was always sheer agony. It was a heaven-sent salvation when gas came in.'

My mother went into the dentist's office, where my grandfather was sitting in the chair, white with pain. She asked him if she could have her hair cut. He said she could do anything in tarnation as long as she would get out of there and stop pestering him.

'So I went out straight away and had it all chopped off,' says my mother jauntily. 'He was furious afterwards, but what could he do? He'd given his word.'

My own hair reposes in a cardboard box in a steamer trunk in my mother's cellar, where I picture it becoming duller and more brittle with each passing year, and possibly moth-eaten; by now it will look like the faded wreaths of hair in Victorian funeral jewellery. Or it may have developed a dry mildew; inside its tissue-paper wrappings it glows faintly, in the darkness of the trunk. I suspect my mother has forgotten it's in there. It was cut off, much to my relief, when I was twelve and my sister was born. Before that it was in long curls: 'Otherwise,' says my mother, 'it would have been just one big snarl.' My mother combed it by winding it around her index finger every morning, but when she was in the hospital my father couldn't cope. 'He couldn't get it around his stubby fingers,' says my mother. My father looks down at his fingers. They are indeed broad compared with m mother's long elegant ones, which she calls boney. He smiles a pussy-cat smile.

So it was that my hair was sheared off. I sat in the chair in my first beauty parlour and watched if falling, like handfuls of cobwebs, down over my shoulders. From within it my head began to emerge, smaller, denser, my face more angular. I aged five years in fifteen minutes. I knew I could go home now and try out lipstick.

'Your father was upset about it,' says my mother, with an air of collusion. She doesn't say this when my father is present. We smile, over the odd reactions of men to hair.

I used to think that my mother, in her earlier days, led a life of sustained hilarity and hair-raising adventure. (That was before I realized that she never put in the long stretches of uneventful time that must have made up much of her life: the stories were just the punctuation.) Horses ran away with her, men offered to, she was continually falling out of trees or off the ridgepoles of barns, or nearly being swept out to sea in rip-tides; or, in a more minor vein, suffering acute embarrassment in trying circumstances.

Churches were especially dangerous. 'There was a guest preacher one Sunday,' she says. 'Of course we had to go to church every Sunday. There he was, in full career, preaching hellfire and damnation' – she pounds an invisible pulpit – 'and his full set of false teeth shot out of his mouth – *phoop!* – just like that. Well, he didn't miss a stride. He stuck his hand up and caught them and popped them back into his mouth, and he kept right on, condemning us all to eternal torment. The pew was shaking! The tears were rolling down our faces, and the worst of it was, we were in the front pew, he was looking right at us. But of course we couldn't laugh out loud: father would have given us Hail Columbia.'

Other people's parlours were booby-trapped for her; so were any and all formal social occasions. Zippers sprang apart on her clothes in strategic places, hats were unreliable. The shortage of real elastic during the war demanded constant alertness:

underpants then had buttons, and were more taboo and therefore more significant than they are now. 'There you would be,' she says, 'right on the street, and before you knew it they'd be down around your galoshes. The way to do it was to step out of them with one foot, then kick them up with your other foot and whip them into your purse. I got quite good at it.'

This particular story is told only to a few, but other stories are for general consumption. When she tells them, my mother's face turns to rubber. She takes all the parts, adds the sound effects, waves her hands around in the air. Her eyes gleam, sometimes a little wickedly, for although my mother is sweet and old and a lady, she avoids being a sweet old lady. When people are in danger of mistaking her for one, she flings in something from left field; she refuses to be taken for granted.

But my mother cannot be duped into telling stories when she doesn't want to. If you prompt her, she becomes self-conscious and clams up. Or she will laugh and go out into the kitchen, and shortly after that you will hear the whir of the Mixmaster. Long ago I gave up attempting to make her do tricks at parties. In gatherings of unknown people, she merely listens intently, her head tilted a little, smiling a smile of glazed politeness. The secret is to wait and see what she will say afterwards.

*   *   *

At the age of seventeen my mother went to the Normal School in Truro. This name – 'Normal School' – once held a certain magic for me. I thought it had something to do with learning to be normal, which possibly it did, because really it was where you used to go to learn how to be a schoolteacher. Subsequently my mother taught in a one-room school house not far from her home. She rode her horse to and from the school house every day, and saved up the money she earned and sent herself to university with it. My grandfather wouldn't send her: he said she was too frivolous-minded. She liked ice-skating and dancing too much for his taste.

At Normal School my mother boarded with a family tha

contained several sons in more or less the same age group as the girl boarders. They all ate around a huge dining-room table (which I pictured as being of dark wood, with heavy carved legs, but covered always with a white linen tablecloth), with the mother and father presiding, one at each end. I saw them both as large and pink and beaming.

'The boys were great jokers,' says my mother. 'They were always up to something.' This was desirable in boys: to be great jokers, to be always up to something. My mother adds a key sentence: 'We had a lot of fun.'

Having fun has always been high on my mother's agenda. She has as much fun as possible, but what she means by this phrase cannot be understood without making an adjustment, an allowance for the great gulf across which this phrase must travel before it reaches us. It comes from another world, which, like the stars that originally sent out the light we see hesitating in the sky above us these nights, may be or is already gone. It is possible to reconstruct the facts of this world – the furniture, the clothing, the ornaments on the mantelpiece, the jugs and basins and even the chamber-pots in the bedrooms, but not the emotions, not with the same exactness. So much that is now known and felt must be excluded.

This was a world in which guileless flirtation was possible, because there were many things that were simply not done by nice girls, and more girls were nice then. To fall from niceness was to fall not only from grace: sexual acts, by girls at any rate, had financial consequences. Life was more joyful and innocent then, and at the same time permeated with guilt and terror, or at least the occasions for them, on the most daily level. It was like the Japanese haiku: a limited form, rigid in its perimeters, within which an astonishing freedom was possible.

There are photographs of my mother at this time, taken with three or four other girls, linked arm in arm or with their arms thrown jestingly around each other's necks. Behind them, beyond the sea or the hills or whatever is in the background, is a world already hurtling towards ruin, unknown to them: the theory of relativity has been discovered, acid is accumulating at the roots of trees, the bull-frogs are doomed. But they smile with something that from this distance you could almost call gallantry, their right legs thrust forward in parody of a chorus line.

One of the great amusements for the girl boarders and the sons of the family was amateur theatre. Young people – they were called 'young people' – frequently performed in plays which were put on in the church basement. My mother was a regular actor. (I have a stack of the scripts somewhere about the house, yellowing little booklets with my mother's parts checked in pencil. They are all comedies, and all impenetrable.) 'There was no television then,' says my mother. 'You made your own fun.'

For one of these plays a cat was required, and my mother and one of the sons borrowed the family cat. They put it into a canvas bag and drove to the rehearsal (there were cars by then), with my mother holding the cat on her lap. The cat, which must have been frightened, wet itself copiously, through the canvas bag and all over my mother's skirt. At the same time it made the most astonishingly bad smell.

'I was ready to sink through the floorboards,' says my mother. 'But what could I do? All I could do was sit there. In those days things like that' – she means cat pee, or pee of any sort – 'were not mentioned.' She means in mixed company.

I think of my mother driven through the night, skirts dripping, overcome with shame, the young man beside her staring straight ahead, pretending not to notice anything. They both feel that this act of unmentionable urination has been done, not by the cat, but by my mother. And so they continue, in a straight line that takes them over the Atlantic and past the curvature of the earth, out through the moon's orbit and into the dark reaches beyond.

Meanwhile, back on earth, my mother says: 'I had to throw the skirt out. It was a good skirt, too, but nothing could get rid of the smell.

'I only heard your father swear once,' says my mother. My mother herself never swears. When she comes to a place in a story in which swearing is called for, she says 'dad-ratted' or 'blankety-blank.'

'It was when he mashed his thumb, when he was sinking the well, for the pump.' This story, I know, takes place before I was born, up north, where there is nothing underneath the trees and their sheddings but sand and bedrock. The well was for a hand pump, which in turn was the first of the many cabins and houses my parents built together. But since I witnessed later wells being sunk and later hand pumps being installed, I know how it's done. There's a pipe with a point at one end. You pound it into the ground with a sledge-hammer, and as it goes down you screw other lengths of pipe onto it, until you hit drinkable water. To keep from ruining the thread on the top end, you hold a block of wood between the sledge-hammer and the pipe. Better, you get someone else to hold it for you. This is how my father mashed his thumb: he was doing both the holding and the hammering himself.

'It swelled up like a radish,' says my mother. 'He had to make a hole in the nail, with his toad-sticker, to ease the pressure. The blood spurted out like pips from a lemon. Later on the whole nail turned purple and black and dropped off. Luckily he grew another one. They say you only get two chances. When he did it though, he turned the air blue for yards around. I didn't even know he knew those words. I don't know where he picked them up.' She speaks as if these words are a minor contagious disease, like chicken-pox.

Here my father looks modestly down at his plate. For him, there are two worlds: one containing ladies, in which you do not use certain expressions, and another one – consisting of logging camps and other haunts of his youth, and of gatherings of acceptable sorts of men – in which you do. To let the men's world slip over verbally into the ladies' would reveal you as a mannerless boor, but to carry the ladies' world over into the men's brands you a prig and maybe even a pansy. This is the word for it. All of this is well understood between them.

This story illustrates several things: that my father is no pansy, for one; and that my mother behaved properly by being suitably shocked. But my mother's eyes shine with delight while she tells this story. Secretly, she thinks it funny that my father got caught out, even if only once. The thumbnail that fell off is, in any significant way, long forgotten.

There are some stories which my mother does not tell when there are men present: never at dinner, never at parties. She tells them to women only, usually in the kitchen, when they or we are helping with the dishes or shelling peas, or taking the tops and tails off the string beans, or husking corn. She tells them in a lowered voice, without moving her hands around in the air, and they contain no sound effects. These are stories of romantic betrayals, unwanted pregnancies, illnesses of various horrible kinds, marital infidelities, mental breakdowns, tragic suicides, unpleasant lingering deaths. They are not rich in detail or embroidered with incident: they are stark and factual. The women, their own hands moving among the dirty dishes or the husks of vegetables, nod solemnly.

Some of these stories, it is understood, are not to be passed on to my father, because they would upset him. It is well known that women can deal with this sort of thing better than men can. Men are not to be told anything they might find too painful; the secret depths of human nature, the sordid physicalities, might over-whelm or damage them. For instance, men often faint at the sight of their own blood, to which they are not accustomed. For this reason you should never stand behind one in the line at the Red Cross donor clinic. Men, for some mysterious reason, find life more difficult than women do. (My mother believes this, despite the female bodies, trapped, diseased, disappearing, or abandoned, that litter her stories.) Men must be allowed to play in the sandbox of their choice, as happily as they can, without disturbance; otherwise they get cranky and won't eat their dinners. There are all kinds of things that men are simply not equipped to understand, so why expect it of them? Not everyone shares this belief about men; nevertheless, it has its uses.

'She dug up the shrubs from around the house,' says my mother. This story is about a shattered marriage: seriou business. My mother's eyes widen. The other women lean forward. 'All she left him were the shower curtains.' There is a collective sigh, an expelling of breath. My father enters the kitchen, wondering when the tea will be ready, and the women close ranks, turning to him their deceptive blankly smiling faces. Soon afterwards, my mother emerges from the kitchen, carrying the teapot, and sets it down on the table in its ritual place.

'I remember the time we almost died,' says my mother. Many of her stories begin this way. When she is in a certain mood, we are to understand that our lives have been preserved only by a series of amazing coincidences and strokes of luck; otherwise the entire family, individually or collectively, would be dead as doornails. These stories, in addition to producing adrenalin, serve to reinforce our sense of gratitude. There is the time we almost went over a waterfall, in a canoe, in a fog; the time we almost got caught in a forest fire; the time my father almost got squashed, before my mother's very eyes, by a ridgepole he was lifting into place; the time my brother almost got struck by a bolt of lightning, which went by him so close it knocked him down. 'You could hear it sizzle,' says my mother.

This is the story of the hay wagon. 'Your father was driving,' says my mother, 'at the speed he usually goes.' We read between the lines: *too fast*. 'You kids were in the back.' I can remember this day, so I can remember how old I was, how old my brother was. We were old enough to think it was funny to annoy my father by singing popular songs of a type he disliked, such as 'Mockingbird Hill'; or perhaps we were imitating bagpipe music by holding our noses and humming, while hitting our Adam's apples with the edges of our hands. When we became too irritating my father would say, 'Pipe down.' We weren't old enough to know that his irritation could be real: we thought it was part of the game.

'We were going down a steep hill,' my mother continues, 'when a hay wagon pulled out right across the road, at the bottom. Your father put on the brakes, but nothing happened. The brakes were gone! I thought our last moment had come.'

Luckily the hay wagon continued across the road, and we shot past it, missing it by at least a foot. 'My heart was in my mouth,' says my mother.

I didn't know until afterwards what had really happened. I was in the back seat, making bagpipe music, oblivious. The scenery was the same as it always was on car trips: my parents' heads, seen from behind, sticking up above the front seat. My father had his hat on, the one he wore to keep things from falling off the trees into his hair. My mother's hand was placed lightly on the back of his neck.

'You had such an acute sense of smell when you were younger,' says my mother.

Now we are on more dangerous ground: my mother's childhood is one thing, my own quite another. This is the moment at which I start rattling the silverware, or ask for another cup of tea. 'You used to march into houses that were strange to you, and you would say in a loud voice, "What's that funny smell?" ' If there are guests present, they shift a little away from me, conscious of their own emanations, trying not to look at my nose.

'I used to be so embarrassed,' says my mother absent-mindedly. Then she shifts gears. 'You were such an easy child. You used to get up at six in the morning and play by yourself in the play room, singing away. . . .' There is a pause. A distant voice, mine, high and silvery, drifts over the space between us. 'You used to talk a blue streak. Chatter, chatter, chatter, from morning to night.' My mother sighs imperceptibly, as if wondering why I have become so silent, and gets up to poke the fire.

Hoping to change the subject, I ask whether or not the crocuses have come up yet, but she is not to be diverted. 'I never had to spank you,' she says. 'A harsh word, and you would be completely reduced.' She looks at me sideways; she isn't sure what I have turned into, or how. 'There were just one or two times. Once, when I had to go out and I left your father in charge.' (This may be the real point of the story: the inability c men to second-guess small children.) 'I came back along the street, and there were you and your brother, throwing mud balls at an old man out of the upstairs window.'

We both know whose idea this was. For my mother, the proper construction to be put on this event is that my brother was a hell-raiser and I was his shadow, 'easily influenced,' as my mother puts it. 'You were just putty in his hands.'

'Of course, I had to punish both of you equally,' she says. Of course. I smile a forgiving smile. The real truth is that I was sneakier than my brother, and got caught less often. No front-line charges into enemy machine-gun nests for me, if they could be at all avoided. My own solitary acts of wickedness were devious and well concealed; it was only in partnership with my brother that I would throw caution to the winds.

'He could wind you around his little finger,' says my mother. 'Your father made each of you a toy-box, and the rule was – ' (my mother is good at the devising of rules) ' – the rule was that neither of you could take the toys out of the other one's toy-box without permission. Otherwise he would have got all your toys away from you. But he got them anyway, mind you. He used to talk you into playing house, and he would pretend to be the baby. Then he would pretend to cry, and when you asked what he wanted, he'd demand whatever it was out of your toy-box that he wanted to play with at the moment. You always gave it to him.'

I don't remember this, though I do remember staging World War II on the living-room floor, with armies of stuffed bears and rabbits; but surely some primal patterns were laid down. Have these early toy-box experiences – and 'toy-box' itself, as a concept, reeks with implications – have they made me suspicious of men who wish to be mothered, yet susceptible to them at the same time? Have I been conditioned to believe that if I am not solicitous, if I am not forthcoming, if I am not a never-ending cornucopia of entertaining delights, they will take their collections of milk-bottle tops and their mangy one-eared teddy bears and go away into the woods by themselves to play snipers? Probably. What my mother thinks was merely cute may have been lethal.

But this is not her only story about my suckiness and gullibility. She follows up with the *coup de grâce*, the tale of the bunny-rabbit cookies.

'It was in Ottawa. I was invited to a government tea,' says my mother, and this fact alone should signal an element of horror: my mother hated official functions, to which however she was obliged to go because she was the wife of a civil servant. 'I had to drag you kids along; we couldn't afford a lot of babysitters in those days.' The hostess had made a whole plateful of decorated cookies for whatever children might be present, and my mother proceeds to describe these: wonderful cookies shaped like bunny rabbits, with faces and clothes of coloured icing, little skirts for the little girl bunny rabbits, little pants for the little boy bunny rabbits.

'You chose one,' says my mother. 'You went off to a corner with it, by yourself. Mrs X noticed you and went over. "Aren't you going to eat your cookie?" she said. "Oh, no," you said. "I'll just sit here and talk to it." And there you sat, as happy as a clam. But someone had made the mistake of leaving the plate near your brother. When they looked again, there wasn't a single cookie left. He'd eaten every one. He was very sick that night, I can tell you.'

Some of my mother's stories defy analysis. What is the moral of this one? That I was a simp is clear enough, but on the other hand it was my brother who got the stomach-ache. Is it better to eat your food, in a straightforward materialistic way, and as much of it as possible, or go off into the corner and talk to it? This used to be a favourite of my mother's before I was married, when I would bring what my father referred to as 'swains' home for dinner. Along with the dessert, out would come the bunny-rabbit cookie story, and I would cringe and twiddle my spoon while my mother forged blithely on with it. What were the swains supposed to make of it? Were my kindliness and essential femininity being trotted out for their inspection? Were they being told in a roundabout way that I was harmless, that they could expect to be talked to by me, but not devoured? Or was she, in some way, warning them off? Because there is something faintl crazed about my behaviour, some tinge of the kind of person who might be expected to leap up suddenly from the dinner table and shout, 'Don't eat that! It's alive!'

There is, however, a difference between symbolism and anecdote. Listening to my mother, I sometimes remember this.

'In my next incarnation,' my mother said once, 'I'm going to be an archaeologist and go around digging things up.' We were sitting on the bed that had once been my brother's, then mine, then my sister's; we were sorting out things from one of the trunks, deciding what could now be given away or thrown out. My mother believes that what you save from the past is mostly a matter of choice.

At that time something wasn't right in the family; someone wasn't happy. My mother was angry: her good cheer was not paying off.

This statement of hers startled me. It was the first time I'd ever heard my mother say that she might have wanted to be something other than what she was. I must have been thirty-five at the time, but it was still shocking and slightly offensive to me to learn that my mother might not have been totally contented fulfilling the role in which fate had cast her: that of being my mother. What thumb-suckers we all are, I thought, when it comes to mothers.

Shortly after this I became a mother myself, and this moment altered for me.

While she was combing my next-to-impossible hair, winding it around her long index finger, yanking out the snarls, my mother used to read me stories. Most of them are still in the house somewhere, but one has vanished. It may have been a library book. It was about a little girl who was so poor she had only one potato left for her supper, and while she was roasting it the potato got up and ran away. There was the usual chase, but I can't remember the ending: a significant lapse.

'That story was one of your favourites,' says my mother. She is probably still under the impression that I identified with the little girl, with her hunger and her sense of loss; whereas in reality I identified with the potato.

Early influences are important. It took that one a while to come out; probably until after I went to university and started wearing black stockings and pulling my hair back into a bun, and having pretensions. Gloom set in. Our next-door neighbour, who was interested in wardrobes, tackled my mother: ' "If she would only *do* something about herself," ' my mother quotes, ' "she could be *quite attractive.*" '

'You always kept yourself busy,' my mother says charitably, referring to this time. 'You always had something cooking. Some project or other.'

It is part of my mother's mythology that I am as cheerful and productive as she is, though she admits that these qualities may be occasionally and temporarily concealed. I wasn't allowed much angst around the house. I had to indulge it in the cellar, where my mother wouldn't come upon me brooding and suggest I should go out for a walk, to improve my circulation. This was her answer to any sign, however slight, of creeping despondency. There wasn't a lot that a brisk sprint through dead leaves, howling winds, or sleet couldn't cure.

It was, I knew, the *zeitgeist* that was afflicting me, and against it such simple remedies were powerless. Like smog I wafted through her days, dankness spreading out from around me. I read modern poetry and histories of Nazi atrocities, and took to drinking coffee. Off in the distance, my mother vacuumed around my feet while I sat in chairs, studying, with car rugs tucked around me, for suddenly I was always cold.

My mother has few stories to tell about these times. What I remember from them is the odd look I would sometimes catch in her eyes. It struck me, for the first time in my life, that my mother might be afraid of me. I could not even reassure her, because I was only dimly aware of the nature of her distress, but there must have been something going on in me that was beyond her: at any time I might open my mouth and out would come a language she had never heard before. I had become a visitant from outer space, a time-traveller come back from the future, bearing news of a great disaster.

Father and Son

Bernard Mac Laverty

Because I do not sleep well I hear my father rising to go to work. I know that in a few minutes he will come in to look at me sleeping. He will want to check that I came home last night. He will stand in his bare feet, his shoes and socks in his hand, looking at me. I will sleep for him. Downstairs I hear the snap of the switch on the kettle. I hear him not eating anything, going about the kitchen with a stomach full of wind. He will come again to look at me before he goes out to his work. He will want a conversation. He climbs the stairs and stands breathing through his nose with an empty lunch-box in the crook of his arm, looking at me.

This is my son who let me down. I love him so much it hurts but he won't talk to me. He tells me nothing. I hear him groan and see his eyes flicker open. When he sees me he turns away, a heave of bedclothes in his wake.

'Wake up, son. I'm away to my work. Where are you going today?'
    'What's it to you?'
    'If I know what you're doing I don't worry as much.'
    'Shit.'

I do not sleep. My father does not sleep. The sound of ambulances criss-crosses the dark. I sleep with the daylight. It is safe. At night I hear his bare feet click as he lifts them, walking the lino. The front door shudders as he leaves.

My son is breaking my heart. It is already broken. Is it my fault there is no woman in the house? Is it my fault a good woman should die? His face was never softer than when after I had shaved. A baby pressed to my shaved cheek. Now his chin is sandpaper. He is a man. When he was a boy I took him fishing. I taught him how to tie a blood-knot, how to cast a fly, how to strike so the fish would not escape. How to play a fish. The green bus to quiet days in Toome. Him pestering me with questions. If I leave him alone he will break my heart anyway. I must speak to him. Tonight at tea. If he is in.

'You should be in your bed. A man of your age. It's past one.'
    'Let me make you some tea.'
    The boy shrugs and sits down. He takes up the paper between him and his father.
    'What do you be doing out to this time?'
    'Not again.'
    'Answer me.'
    'Talking.'
    'Who with?'
    'Friends. Just go to bed, Da, will you?'
    'What do you talk about?'
    'Nothing much.'
    'Talk to me, son.'
    'What about?'

My son, he looks confused. I want you to talk to me the way I hear you talk to people at the door. I want to hear you laugh with me like you used to. I want to know what you think. I want to know why you do not eat more. No more than pickings for four weeks. Your face is thin. Your fingers, orange with nicotine. I pulled you away from death once and now you will not talk to me. I want to know if you are in danger again.

'About . . .'
    'You haven't shaved yet.'
    'I'm just going to. The water in the kettle is hot.'
    'Why do you shave at night?'
    'Because in the morning my hand shakes.'

Your hand shakes in the morning, Da, because you're a coward. You think the world is waiting round the corner to blow your head off. A breakfast of two Valium and the rest of them rattling in your pocket, walking down the street to your work. Won't answer the door without looking out the bedroom window first. He's scared of his own shadow.

Son, you are living on borrowed time. Your hand shook when you got home. I have given you the life you now have. I fed you soup from a spoon when your own hand would have spilled it. Let me put my arm around your shoulders and let me listen to what is making you thin. At the weekend I will talk to him.

It is hard to tell if his bed has been slept in. It is always rumpled. I have not seen my son for two days. Then, on the radio, I hear he is dead. They give out his description. I drink milk. I cry.
    But he comes in for his tea.

'Why don't you tell me where you are?'
    'Because I never know where I am.'

My mother is dead but I have another one in her place. He is an old woman. He has been crying. I know he prays for me all the time. He used to dig the garden, grow vegetables and flowers for half the street. He used to fish. To take me fishing. Now he just waits. He sits and waits for me and the weeds have taken over. I would like to slap his face and make a man out of him.

'I let you go once – and look what happened.'
    'Not this again.'
    The boy curls his lip as if snagged on a fish-hook.

For two years I never heard a scrape from you. I read of London in the papers. Watched scenes from London on the news, looking over the reporter's shoulder at people walking in the street. I know you, son, you are easily led. Then a doctor phoned for me at work. The poshest man I ever spoke to.
    'I had to go and collect you. Like a dog.'

The boy had taken up a paper. He turns the pages noisily, crackling like fire.

'A new rig-out from Littlewoods.'

Socks, drawers, shirt, the lot. In a carrier-bag. The doctor said he had to burn what was on you. I made you have your girl's hair cut. It was Belfast before we spoke. You had the taint of England in your voice.

'Today I thought you were dead.'

Every day you think I am dead. You live in fear. Of your own death. Peeping behind curtains, the radio always loud enough to drown any noise that might frighten you, double locking doors. When you think I am not looking you hold your stomach. You undress in the dark for fear of your shadow falling on the window-blind. At night you lie with the pillow over your head. By your bed a hatchet which you pretend to have forgotten to tidy away. Mice have more courage.

'Well I'm not dead.'

'Why don't you tell me where you go?'

'Look, Da, I have not touched the stuff since I came back. Right?'

'Why don't you have a girl like everybody else?'

'Oh fuck.'

He bundles the paper and hurls it in the corner and stamps up the stairs to his room. The old man shouts at the closed door.

'Go and wash your mouth out.'

He cries again, staring at the ceiling so that the tears run down to his ears.

My son, he is full of hatred. For me, for everything. He spits when he speaks. When he shouts his voice breaks high and he is like a woman. He grinds his teeth and his skin goes white about his mouth. His hands shake. All because I ask him where he goes. Perhaps I need to show him more love. Care for him more than I do.

I mount the stairs quietly to apologize. My son, I am sorry. I do it because I love you. Let me put my arm around you and talk like we used to on the bus from Toome. Why do you fight away from me?

The door swings open and he pushes a hand-gun beneath the pillow. Seen long enough, black and squat, dull like a garden slug. He sits, my son, his hands idling empty, staring hatred.

'Why do you always spy on me, you nosey old bastard?' His voice breaks, his eyes bulge.

'What's that? Under your pillow?'

'It's none of your business.'

He kicks the door closed in my face with his bare foot.

I am in the dark of the landing. I must pray for him. On my bended knees I will pray for him to be safe. Perhaps I did not see what I saw. Maybe I am mistaken. My son rides pillion on a motor-bike. Tonight I will not sleep. I do not think I will sleep again.

It is ten o'clock. The news begins. Like a woman I stand drying a plate, watching the headlines. There is a ring at the door. The boy answers it, his shirt-tail out. Voices in the hallway.

My son with friends. Talking. What he does not do with me.

There is a bang. A dish-cloth drops from my hand and I run to the kitchen door. Not believing, I look into the hallway. There is a strange smell. My son is lying on the floor, his head on the bottom stair, his feet on the threshold. The news has come to my door. The house is open to the night. There is no one else. I go to him with damp hands.

'Are you hurt?'

Blood is spilling from his nose.

They have punched you and you are not badly hurt. Your nose is bleeding. Something cold at the back of your neck.

I take my son's limp head in my hands and see a hole in his nose that should not be there. At the base of his nostril.

My son, let me put my arms around you.

In the Cutting of a Drink

Ama Ata Aidoo

I say, my uncles, if you are going to Accra and anyone tells you that the best place for you to drop down is at the Circle, then he has done you good, but . . . Hm . . . I even do not know how to describe it. . . .

'Are all these beings that are passing this way and that way human? Did men buy all these cars with money . . .?'

But my elders, I do not want to waste your time. I looked round and did not find my bag. I just fixed my eyes on the ground and walked on. . . . Do not ask me why. Each time I tried to raise my eyes, I was dizzy from the number of cars which were passing. And I could not stand still. If I did, I felt as if the whole world was made up of cars in motion. There is something somewhere, my uncles. Not desiring to deafen you with too long a story . . .

I stopped walking just before I stepped into the Circle itself. I stood there for a long time. Then a lorry came along and I beckoned to the driver to stop. Not that it really stopped.

'Where are you going?' he asked me.

'I am going to Mamprobi,' I replied. 'Jump in,' he said, and he started to drive away. Hm . . . I nearly fell down climbing in. As we went round the thing which was like a big bowl on a very huge stump of wood, I had it in mind to have a good look at it, and later Duayaw told me that it shoots water in the air . . . but the driver was talking to me, so I could not look at it properly. He told me he himself was not going to Mamprobi but he was going to the station where I could take a lorry which would be going there. . . .

Yes, my uncle, he did not deceive me. Immediately we arrived at the station I found the driver of a lorry shouting 'Mamprobi, Mamprobi'. Finally when the clock struck about two-thirty, I

125

was knocking on the door of Duayaw. I did not knock for long when the door opened. Ah, I say, he was fast asleep, fast asleep I say, on a Saturday afternoon.

'How can folks find time to sleep on Saturday afternoons?' I asked myself. We hailed each other heartily. My uncles, Duayaw has done well for himself. His mother Nsedua is a very lucky woman.

How is it some people are lucky with school and others are not? Did not Mansa go to school with Duayaw here in this very school which I can see for myself? What have we done that Mansa should have wanted to stop going to school?

But I must continue with my tale. . . . Yes, Duayaw has done well for himself. His room has fine furniture. Only it is too small. I asked him why and he told me he was even lucky to have got that narrow place that looks like a box. It is very hard to find a place to sleep in the city. . . .

He asked me about the purpose of my journey. I told him everything. How, as he himself knew, my sister Mansa had refused to go to school after 'Klase Tri' and how my mother had tried to persuade her to go . . .

My mother, do not interrupt me, everyone present here knows you tried to do what you could by your daughter.

Yes, I told him how, after she had refused to go, we finally took her to this woman who promised to teach her to keep house and to work with the sewing-machine . . . and how she came home the first Christmas after the woman took her but has never been home again, these twelve years.

Duayaw asked me whether it was my intention then to look for my sister in the city. I told him yes. He laughed saying, 'You are funny. Do you think you can find a woman in this place? You do not know where she is staying. You do not even know whether she is married or not. Where can we find her if someone big has married her and she is now living in one of those big bungalows which are some ten miles from the city?'

Do you cry 'My Lord', mother? You are surprised about what I said about the marriage? Do not be. I was surprised too, when he talked that way. I too cried 'My Lord' . . . Yes, I too did, mother. But you and I have forgotten that Mansa was born a girl and girls do not take much time to grow. We are thinking of her as we last saw her when she was ten years old. But mother, that is twelve years ago . . .

Yes, Duayaw told me that she is by now old enough to marry and to do something more than merely marry. I asked him whether he knew where she was and if he knew whether she had any children – 'Children?' he cried, and he started laughing, a certain laugh. . . .

I was looking at him all the time he was talking. He told me he was not just discouraging me but he wanted me to see how big and difficult it was, what I proposed to do. I replied that it did not matter. What was necessary was that even if Mansa was dead, her ghost would know that we had not forgotten her entirely. That we had not let her wander in other people's towns and that we had tried to bring her home. . . .

These are useless tears you have started to weep, my mother. Have I said anything to show that she was dead?

Duayaw and I decided on the little things we would do the following day as the beginning of our search. Then he gave me water for my bath and brought me food. He sat by me while I ate and asked me for news of home. I told him that his father has married another woman and of how last year the *akatse* spoiled all our cocoa. We know about that already. When I finished eating, Duayaw asked me to stretch out my bones on the bed and I did. I think I slept fine because when I opened my eyes it was dark. He had switched on his light and there was a woman in the room. He showed me her as a friend but I think she is the girl he wants to marry against the wishes of his people. She is as beautiful as sunrise, but she does not come from our parts . . .

When Duayaw saw that I was properly awake, he told me it had struck eight o'clock in the evening and his friend had brought some food. The three of us ate together.

Do not say 'Ei', uncle, it seems as if people do this thing in the city. A woman prepares a meal for a man and eats it with him. Yes, they do so often.

My mouth could not manage the food. It was prepared from

cassava and corn dough, but it was strange food all the same. I tried to do my best. After the meal, Duayaw told me we were going for a night out. It was then I remembered my bag. I told him that as matters stood, I could not change my cloth and I could not go out with them. He would not hear of it. 'It would certainly be a crime to come to this city and not go out on a Saturday night.' He warned me though that there might not be many people, or anybody at all, where we were going who would also be in cloth but I should not worry about that.

Cut me a drink, for my throat is very dry, my uncle. . . .

When we were on the street, I could not believe my eyes. The whole place was as clear as the sky. Some of these lights are very beautiful indeed. Everyone should see them . . . and there are so many of them! 'Who is paying for all these lights?' I asked myself. I could not say that aloud for fear Duayaw would laugh.

We walked through many streets until we came to a big building where a band was playing. Duayaw went to buy tickets for the three of us.

You all know that I had not been to anywhere like that before. You must allow me to say that I was amazed. 'Ei, are all these people children of human beings? And where are they going? And what do they want?'

Before I went in, I thought the building was big, but when I went in, I realized the crowd in it was bigger. Some were in front of a counter buying drinks, others were dancing . . .

Yes, that was the case, uncle, we had gone to a place where they had given a dance, but I did not know.

Some people were sitting on iron chairs around iron tables. Duayaw told some people to bring us a table and chairs and they did. As soon as we sat down, Duayaw asked us what we would drink. As for me, I told him *lamlale* but his woman asked for 'Beer' . . .

Do not be surprised, uncles.

Yes, I remember very well, she asked for beer. It was not long before Duayaw brought them. I was too surprised to drink mine. I sat with my mouth open and watched the daughter of a woman 'ıt beer like a man. The band had stopped playing for some time and soon they started again. Duayaw and his woman went to dance. I sat there and drank my *lamlale*. I cannot describe how they danced.

After some time, the band stopped playing and Duayaw and his woman came to sit down. I was feeling cold and I told Duayaw. He said, 'And this is no wonder, have you not been drinking this women's drink all the time?'

'Does it make one cold?' I asked him.

'Yes,' he replied. 'Did you not know that? You must drink beer.'

'Yes,' I replied. So he bought me beer. When I was drinking the beer, he told me I would be warm if I danced.

'You know I cannot dance the way you people dance,' I told him.

'And how do we dance?' he asked me.

'I think you all dance like white men and as I do not know how that is done, people would laugh at me,' I said. Duayaw started laughing. He could not contain himself. He laughed so much his woman asked him what it was all about. He said something in the white man's language and they started laughing again. Duayaw then told me that if people were dancing, they would be so busy that they would not have time to watch others dance. And also, in the city, no one cares if you dance well or not . . .

Yes, I danced too, my uncles. I did not know anyone, that is true. My uncle, do not say that instead of concerning myself with the business for which I had gone to the city, I went dancing. Oh, if you only knew what happened at this place, you would not be saying this. I would not like to stop somewhere and tell you the end . . . I would rather like to put a rod under the story, as it were, clear off every little creeper in the bush . . .

But as we were talking about the dancing, something made Duayaw turn to look behind him where four women were sitting by the table. . . . Oh! he turned his eyes quickly, screwed his face into something queer which I could not understand and told me that if I wanted to dance, I could ask one of those women to dance with me.

My uncles, I too was very surprised when I heard that. I asked

Duayaw if people who did not know me would dance with me. He said 'Yes.' I lifted my eyes, my uncles, and looked at those four young women sitting round a table alone. They were sitting all alone, I say. I got up.

I hope I am making myself clear, my uncles, but I was trembling like water in a brass bowl.

Immediately one of them saw me, she jumped up and said something in that kind of white man's language which everyone, even those who have not gone to school, speak in the city. I shook my head. She said something else in the language of the people of the place. I shook my head again. Then I heard her ask me in Fante whether I wanted to dance with her. I replied 'Yes.'

Ei! my little sister, are you asking me a question? Oh! you want to know whether I found Mansa? I do not know. . . . Our uncles have asked me to tell everything that happened there, and you too! I am cooking the whole meal for you, why do you want to lick the ladle now?

Yes, I went to dance with her. I kept looking at her so much I think I was all the time stepping on her feet. I say, she was as black as you and I, but her hair was very long and fell on her shoulders like that of a white woman. I did not touch it but I saw it was very soft. Her lips with that red paint looked like a fresh wound. There was no space between her skin and her dress. Yes, I danced with her. When the music ended, I went back to where I was sitting. I do not know what she told her companions about me, but I heard them laugh.

It was this time that something made me realize that they were all bad women of the city. Duayaw had told me I would feel warm if I danced, yet after I had danced, I was colder than before. You would think someone had poured water on me. I was unhappy thinking about these women. 'Have they no homes?' I asked myself. 'Do not their mothers like them? God, we are all toiling for our threepence to buy something to eat . . . but oh! God! this is no work.'

When I thought of my own sister, who was lost, I became a little happy because I felt that although I had not found her, she was nevertheless married to a big man and all was well with her.

When they started to play the band again, I went to the women's table to ask the one with whom I had danced to dance again. But someone had gone with her already. I got one of the two who were still sitting there. She went with me. When we were dancing she asked me whether it was true that I was a Fante. I replied 'Yes.' We did not speak again. When the band stopped playing, she told me to take her to where they sold things to buy her beer and cigarettes. I was wondering whether I had the money. When we were where the lights were shining brightly, something told me to look at her face. Something pulled at my heart.

'Young woman, is this the work you do?' I asked her.

'Young man, what work do you mean?' she too asked me. I laughed.

'Do you not know what work?' I asked again.

'And who are you to ask me such questions? I say, who are you? Let me tell you that any kind of work is work. You villager, you villager, who are you?' she screamed.

I was afraid. People around were looking at us. I laid my hands on her shoulders to calm her down and she hit them away.

'Mansa, Mansa,' I said. 'Do you not know me?' She looked at me for a long time and started laughing. She laughed, laughed as if the laughter did not come from her stomach. Yes, as if she was hungry.

'I think you are my brother,' she said. 'Hm.'

Oh, my mother and my aunt, oh, little sister, are you all weeping? As for you women!

What is there to weep about? I was sent to find a lost child. I found her a woman.

Cut me a drink . . .

Any kind of work is work. . . . This is what Mansa told me with a mouth that looked like clotted blood. Any kind of work is work . . . so do not weep. She will come home this Christmas.

My brother, cut me another drink. Any form of work is work . . . is work . . . is work!

In the Kingdom of the Golden Dust

Neil Bissoondath

Are they out there, wandering through the crowd? Watching? Pedro, Miguel, and Tomás?

It is the sun I am most aware of, the sun and the silence. Reinforcing each other. Conspirators of heat and stillness. I notice that I notice the sand that hangs in the air with the thickness of disturbed dust. It does not exist in the capital, this gritty, golden fog; but here in my little home town it is how we have come to think of air: as body, as color.

To my right the wooden stage, the small crowd before it motionless: browned faces seized by fatigue and the blankness of a passivity easily assumed. Here and there, the peaked khaki caps and reflective sunglasses of policemen – function, as usual, enigmatic.

Behind them the square, a rutted expanse the grey of ancient bones; in the middle, rising as if in natural formation, our fountain of the Virgin Mary, water gushing from under her feet and down the hidden pedestal to the pool of unfinished concrete black with moisture.

In the distance the western limit of the square: a line of flat-roofed, one-storey buildings a shade or two lighter than the sand of the square, weathered outgrowths with windows shuttered to the heat.

And above, above it all, in a sweep so total it suffocates, thunders a sky of a blue faded as if bleached by the sun.

And all this, all this before me, stilled by the tension that sits massively in my lower stomach, idling, consuming.

A stirring behind me. The others girls – we are ten in all, I the oldest at sixteen – shuffle with a tinge of fear, make way for Lisímaco Gonzalez. As usual he is wearing his police uniform, the khaki shirt, long unwashed, showing consecutive rings of perspiration stains beneath the arms. As he walks past us, short, gaunt, smiling, he says: 'Girls . . .'

He drags out the *s*, and the simple word, offered in greeting, is like a statement of possession: Girls . . .

He mounts the stairs to the stage, pauses at the top, and looks back down at us: His black eyes, round and with a dull shine, never focusing, like a statue with the eyes painted in, squint at us in contemplation; then, quickly, impatience: 'Come,' he says, 'come.' His right hand, palm upwards, flicks rapidly at the wrist, urging us to follow him: 'You are the stars, not me.'

The girls gather around me: I am the eldest, they come to me as to a leader.

'What are you waiting for, Maria Luisa?' says Lisímaco Gonzalez. 'Come.'

I mount the first step and he reaches down as if to help me up; but his fingers strap themselves firmly around my wrist: not help this, but seizure. I gasp from the jolt of pain that slices along my forearm. He pulls me up to him, takes my left arm in his hand – the grip still that of the policeman – and looks down at the others: 'Come.'

Slowly they follow me up. Lisímaco Gonzalez has us form a line across the middle of the stage, facing the crowd; then he addresses those faces tense with retreated eyes: 'Dear friends . . .'

I look beyond him, sending my gaze to the distance, past the Virgin Mary, to the buildings that, from here, just a few feet above the ground, shimmer in the yellow mist: surely they are out there somewhere, Pedro, Miguel, and Tomás? I try to picture their faces but cannot, still, not since that morning three months ago. My eyes water, stung by the dust.

'And now our first contestant,' says Lisímaco Gonzalez. He half turns and motions Consuelo to him from the end of the line. The golden dust swirls and eddies at the flap of his hand.

And through that movement, for just a few seconds, so few that I know immediately that it is but a trick of the light, I see among the crowd that other face: young and angular, cheeks smooth with boyishness, thin lips compressed beneath pencil strokes of hair, dead eyes shining dully from the shadow cast on the upper half of his face by the lip of his green helmet.

Those tightened lips – twitching at the corners as if with suppressed laughter the morning of the *mistake*, his word, not mine – come back to me. I remember how he turned his face, mask-like, towards me; how that tightness slipped for a brief moment into a smile. And the horror of that moment, a horror that went well beyond that which had already seized me, comes afresh, like slivers of ice scorching through my stomach.

'And now, contestant number two,' says Lisímaco Gonzalez.

Consuelo returns to her place in the line.

Rafaela, hesitant, in the plain white dress I associate with funerals and festivals, makes her way over to Lisímaco Gonzalez.

From above, the yellow heat deepens, thickens, caking itself onto my face with the grainy dryness of dead earth.

Lisímaco Gonzalez' right arm encircles Rafaela's waist. It is a gesture I know: friendly from a distance, lightly abusive closer up. I feel for Rafaela, know her confusion, see the tension in her neck between the braids that hang down to each of her shoulders.

Then I notice the little red ribbons with which she has secured the knots of the braids and I feel even more for her. This little protest: the snatch of colour that neither screams nor whimpers, but that registers with a subtlety that is like love.

Lisímaco Gonzalez sends Rafaela back to the line and, half-turned, gestures at me. The flapping hand, impatient, like a large, dead leaf flicked at by the wind, tugs at me through the visible air.

Dust swirls.

A hand pushes insistently at my lower back, urging me forward – who? Not Rafaela. Angela, to my left. I slap her hand away and, instantly, I regret my sharpness. Hers is a fear I understand.

The dust thickens before my eyes in a sudden distillation, It is like that other morning: The scene of the *mistake* – the buildings, the faces, the soldiers with guns – remains with me through a milky film, like seeing the world through glasses long uncleaned.

I move forward, towards Lisímaco Gonzalez, but it is not like walking. I do not feel the stage beneath me; I feel myself insubstantial.

'How old are you, Maria Luisa?'

'Seventeen.'

The faces of the crowd look up at me: unreadable. Do they feel what I feel? Do they see my shame?

'You write poetry?'

'Yes.'

'What do you write about?'

'Anything.'

'Flowers? Birds?'

'Yes.'

And murder, I want to add.

'And right now you are taking a little holiday from your studies in the capital?'

'Yes.'

'What are you studying?'

'Typing.'

And then, at the back of the crowd, standing side by side, silent and motionless, obscured by the dust and sun: Pedro, Miguel, and Tomás.

'You are going to become a secretary?'

'Yes.'

Pedro, Miguel, and Tomás!

But where are they now?

Gone. Again.

'A secretary, friends! Sec-re-ta-ry! And this, by the grace of God, from our government, Maria Luisa?'

'No. The missionaries. The Canadians.'

There is pause, and I feel his confusion. For this brief moment, his control is gone.

'Some applause, friends! Applause for our Maria Luisa!'

Hands move in the crowd. The golden air swirls.

Then, once more, I see them: Pedro, Miguel, and Tomás.

And then I don't.

The sun. The sun.

I move back to the line, still searching the crowd: They must be playing, hiding from me behind the backs of the people.

Angela, moving forward, bumps into me, startles me. I yelp. Lisímaco Gonzalez smiles. And my ears tell me I have made a sound of delight: My shame rises, hot, to my face.

Rafaela puts her arm through mine. 'You are sweating, Maria Luisa.'

'Pedro, Miguel, and Tomás, they are here, Rafaela.'

She pulls her arm away. 'No, Maria Luisa, they are dead.'

'I saw them. In the crowd.'

'Not them, Maria Luisa. Lieutenant Morales, yes, he is out there.'

'You too have seen him, then?'

'He was there. In his helmet.'

'Then they too are here.'

'Morales is not dead, Maria.'

'But they go with him. Where he is, they are.'

I search the crowd, eyes darting this way and that. They are out there, I am sure, playing with me.

Pedro, Miguel, and Tomás.

In the heat. The terrible heat.

Time suspended in a dense solution of heat and golden dust.

My skin itches, forehead aches; air whistles through my clogged nostrils.

Before me nothing moves. Lisímaco Gonzalez, drooping, khaki shirt blackened with sweat, beside him Estela, the last of his contest. The crowd immobile; the Holy Virgin, always stilled, on her column of crystal.

Only the buildings defy, shimmering like reflections in disturbed water, behind and above them the huge, empty sky exploding in a nothingness of virgin blue.

A movement on the stage in front of me: forms, rounded shapes in a pile.

And there they are: Pedro, Miguel, and Tomás. Lying at my feet.

Pedro, on his back, head tilted away from me, hands resting as if in contentment on his stomach, right ankle thrown casually over left ankle, soccer boots muddied as with chocolate icing.

Miguel, face downwards, arms flung out to either side, a rug of blood, dark crimson, creeping out from under his chest.

Tomás, head resting on Miguel's legs, staring up glassy-eyed at me, brain hanging from the hole in the left side of his head, mouth echoing voiceless screams.

Slowly Pedro, eyes closed, turns his head towards me and smiles.

Miguel gathers in his arms, turns on his side so that blood and bits of flesh gush from the hole in his chest, smiles and opens his eyes, ovals of coral white, then hops to his feet. His litheness surprises me. Beneath him is their soccer ball, flattened and soaked in blood, an oval in black and red.

Tomás's lips close and widen, tightening into his thin smile. Stiffly, he gets to his feet, the brain jiggling and excreting a green liquid that flows into his blood-matted hair, over his ear and onto his shoulder.

Pedro, lying still, says, 'Hi, Maria Luisa. We had you fooled, didn't we? You thought we weren't coming back, didn't you?'

Tomás says: 'We were just playing soccer, Maria Luisa, don't be angry.'

Miguel says: 'We must practise, all the time. Practise, practise, practise!'

Pedro and Miguel chant: 'Practise, practise, practise!'

Now they are all around me, ripped, bloodied, talking all at the same time, with one voice yet with different voices, voices I seem to know but am not sure of knowing.

'You look beautiful, Maria Luisa.'

'You were born to be a queen, Maria Luisa.'

'The police queen!'

'Even just for one day.'
'We hope the crown won't be too heavy, Maria Luisa.'
'We have a gift for you.'
'To congratulate you.'
'We *know* you will win, Maria Luisa.'
'For the queen.'
'The police queen!'
Tomás says: 'Close your eyes.'
I close my eyes.
'Put out your hands.'

I put out my hands, palms up. The gift, heavy, of warm metal, fills both my hands. I recognize the feel of it, know its shape; and the knowledge of its power suffuses my flesh.

It was before the soldiers came. The boys, dirty and shabby, in the mismatched greens of stolen jungle garb, had spent a week in our town, eating, resting, cleaning their weapons. A young fighter hardly older than I, younger, it seems to me, than the Lieutenant Morales who would come with his men soon after to secure the town for the government, had shown me his weapon. 'It is an AK 47,' he had said, pointing out the strange markings, 'Russian.' And we had both marvelled that anyone could read so curious a language; and we had agreed that anyone who could had to be strange and, in a way we could not grasp, wonderful.

I open my eyes. This dust, this dust that puts me in mind of ground gold.

Pedro, Miguel, and Tomás are gone.

In my hands the AK 47: scarred wooden stock, tubes and protrusions of grey metal.

To my sides, my friends, my competitors, brown faces oiled and shining, eyes glazed by the immobilizing heat.

And before me, caught in the thickness of heat and dust, the sky, the buildings, the Virgin Mary, the crowd, and, in drenched khaki, Lisímaco Gonzalez.

He is talking to the crowd. His words do not carry, fall heavily to his feet.

But I do not need his words to know what he is saying, for Lisímaco Gonzalez is doing his job, serving powers in the capital that he will never know, never understand. The killing will get done, and the only true difficulty is to remember who is to be killed when the orders come to kill.

I think this is why I hate him, why I lower the weapon at him, why I squeeze the trigger and watch with emotions inert as a line of holes stitches itself rapidly across his back, from left to right, little roses with centres of black.

He turns, smiling: large teeth whitened by the squinting darkness of the eyes. In his hands, a small silver trophy and a cardboard crown wrapped in tinfoil. He approaches me, growing larger, blocking out the crowd.

The sun pours down, heat heating heat in a golden mist.

He stands in front of me, exuding a salty mustiness.

The crown on my head.

The trophy in my hands.

And an embrace: hot breath, cigarette smoke, and the stench of fresh perspiration.

A kiss: the right cheek, the left cheek. The lips linger, part, the tip of the tongue traces wetly across my skin.

A lizard, I see a lizard.

He pulls away. At last. And from where his tongue has touched, taking with it the taste of my sweat, rises steam, a steam that is my shame made visible.

'Wave,' he says, 'wave to the people. You are the queen. The police queen.'

I raise my right hand.

The crowd, hesitating, urged on by Lisímaco Gonzalez, begins to applaud. Palms meet and separate, slowly, soundlessly, noise absorbed into the thick air.

Suddenly the trophy in my left hand moves. It becomes soft and pliable, melting, as if about to flow away, metal moving with life inexplicably acquired.

I grasp at it, with both hands now, to support it, to contain it. Quickly it lengthens, hardens, acquires weight, a form twice familiar. My eyes run slowly across the angular lettering, more familiar now but wondrous yet, inscribed in the grey metal.

I look up, past the silently applauding crowd, past the Holy

Virgin in the square, past the buildings into the sky, into the sun.

And in the moment before I have to turn away, when my eyelids seal themselves and a sparkling darkness fills my head, they come to me, Pedro, Miguel, and Tomás, eyebrows raised in amusement, speaking as one words unintelligible with a sound harsh and fantastic, an eager and magical music that sings of things as yet unimagined from a place that remains well beyond imagination, far, far beyond my kingdom of the golden dust.

Learning to Fly

Christopher Hope

Long ago, in the final days of the old regime, there lived a colonel who held an important job in the State Security Police and his name was Rocco du Preez. Colonel du Preez was in charge of the interrogation of political suspects and because of his effect on the prisoners of the old regime he became widely known in the country as 'Window jumpin'' du Preez. After mentioning his name it was customary to add 'thank God', because he was a strong man and in the dying days of the old regime everyone agreed that we needed a strong man. Now Colonel du Preez acquired his rather strange nickname not because he did any window jumping himself but rather because he had been the first to draw attention to this phenomenon which affected so many of the prisoners who were brought before him.

The offices of State Security were situated on the thirteenth floor of a handsome and tall modern block in the centre of town. Their high windows looked down onto a little dead-end street far below. Once this street had been choked with traffic and bustling with thriving shops. Then one day the first jumper landed on the roof of a car parked in the street and after that it was shut to traffic and turned into a pedestrian shopping mall. The street was filled in and covered over with crazy paving and one or two benches set up for weary shoppers. However, the jumpings increased. There were sometimes one or two a week and several nasty accidents on the ground began to frighten off the shoppers.

Whenever a jump had taken place the little street was cordoned off to allow in the emergency services: the police, the undertaker's men, the municipal workers brought in to ho down the area of impact which was often surprisingly large. The jumpings were bad for business and the shopkeepers grew desperate. The authorities were sympathetic and erected covered walk-ways running the length of the street leaving only the central area of crazy pavings and the benches, on which no one had ever been known to sit, exposed to the heavens: the walk-ways protected by their overhead concrete parapets were guaranteed safe against any and all flying objects. But still trade dwindled as one by one the shops closed, and the street slowly died and came to be known by the locals, who gave it a wide berth, as the 'landing field'.

As everyone knows, window jumpings increased apace over the years and being well placed to study them probably led Colonel Rocco du Preez to his celebrated thesis afterwards included in the manual of psychology used by recruits at the Police College and known as du Preez's Law. It states that all men, when brought to the brink, will contrive to find a way out if the least chance is afforded them and the choice of the means is always directly related to the racial characteristics of the individual in question. Some of du Preez's remarks on the subject have come down to us, though these are almost certainly apocryphal, as are so many tales of the final days of the old regime. 'Considering your average white man,' du Preez is supposed to have said, 'my experience is that he prefers hanging – whether by pyjama cord, belt, strips of blanket; providing he finds the handy protuberance, the cell bars, say, or up-ended bedstead, you'll barely have turned your back and he'll be up there swinging from the light cord or some other chosen noose. Your white man in his last throes has a wonderful sense of rhythm – believe me, whatever you may have heard to the contrary – I've seen several Whites about to cough it and all of them have been wonderful dancers. Your Indian, now, he's something else, a slippery customer who prefers smooth surfaces. I've known Asians to slip and crack their skulls in a shower cubicle so narrow you'd have sworn a man couldn't turn in it. This innate slitheriness is probably what makes them good businessmen. Now, your Coloured, per contra, is more clumsy a character altogether. His hidden talent lies in his amazing lack of co-ordination. Even the most sober rogue can appear hopelessly drunk to the untrained eye. On the surface of things it might seem that you can do nothing with him; he has no taste for the knotted strip of blanket or the convenient bootlace; a soapy bathroom floor leaves him unmoved – yet show him a short, steep flight of steps and he instinctively knows what to do. When it comes to Africans I have found that they, perverse as always, choose another way out. They are given to window jumping. This phenomenon has been very widespread in the past few years. Personally, I suspect its roots go back a long way, back to their superstitions – i.e. to their regard for black magic and witchcraft. Everyone knows that in extreme instances your average blackie will believe anything; that his witch-doctors will turn the white man's bullets to water; or, if he jumps out of a window thirteen storeys above terra firma he will miraculously find himself able to fly. Nothing will stop him once his mind's made up. I've seen up to six Bantu jump from a high window on one day. Though the first landed on his head and the others saw the result they were not deterred. It's as if despite the evidence of their senses they believed that if only they could practise enough they would one day manage to take off.'

'Window jumpin'' du Preez worked in an office sparsely furnished with an old desk, a chair, a strip of green, government-issue carpet, a very large steel cabinet marked 'Secret' and a bare, fluorescent light in the ceiling. Poor though the furnishings were, the room was made light and cheerful by the large windows behind his desk and nobody remembers being aware of the meanness of the furnishings when Colonel du Preez was present in the room. When he sat down in his leather swivel chair behind his desk, witnesses reported that he seemed to fill up the room, to make it habitable, even genial. His reddish hair and green eyes were somehow enough to colour the room and make it complete. The eyes had a peculiar, steady glint to them. This was his one peculiarity. When thinking hard about something he had the nervous habit of twirling a lock of the reddish hair, a copper colour with gingery lights, in the words of a witness, around a finger. It was his only nervous habit. Since these were often the last words ever spoken by very brave men, we have to wonder at their ability to register details so sharply under terrible conditions; it is these details that provide us with our only glimpse of the man, as no photographs have come down to us.

It was to this office that three plainclothes men one day brought a new prisoner. The charge-sheet was singularly bare: it read simply. 'Mpahlele. . . Jake. Possession of explosives'. Obviously they had got very little out of him. The men left closing the door softly, almost reverently, behind them.

The prisoner wore an old black coat, ragged grey flannels and a black beret tilted at an angle which gave him an odd, jaunty, rather continental look, made all the more incongruous by the fact that his hands were manacled behind him. Du Preez reached up with his desk ruler and knocked off the beret revealing a bald head gleaming in the overhead fluorescent light. It would have been shaved and polished, du Preez guessed, by one of the wandering barbers who traditionally gathered on Sundays down by the municipal lake, setting up three-legged stools and basins of water and hanging towels and leather strops for their cut-throat razors from the lower branches of a convenient tree and draping their customers in large red and white check cloths, giving them little hand mirrors so that they could look on while the barbers scraped, snipped, polished and gossiped away the sunny afternoon by the water's edge beneath the tall bluegums. Clearly Mpahlele belonged to the old school of whom there were fewer each year as the fashion for Afro-wigs and strange woollen bangs took increasing hold among younger Blacks. Du Preez couldn't help warming to this just a little. After all, he was one of the old school himself in the new age of trimmers and ameliorists. Mpahlele was tall, as tall as du Preez and, he reckoned, about the same age – though it was always difficult to tell with Africans. A knife scar ran from his right eye down to his collar, the flesh fused in a livid welt as if a tiny mole had burrowed under the black skin pushing up a furrow behind it. His nose had been broken, too, probably as the result of the same township fracas, and had mended badly turning to the left and then sharply to the right as if unable to make up its mind. The man was obviously a brawler. Mpahlele's dark brown eyes were remarkably calm – almost to the point of arrogance, du Preez thought for an instant, before dismissing the absurd notion with a tiny smile. It shocked him to see an answering smile on the prisoner's lips. However he was too old a hand to let this show.

'Where are the explosives?'

'I have no explosives,' Mpahlele answered.

He spoke quietly but du Preez thought he detected a most unjustifiable calm amounting to confidence, or worse, to insolence, and he noted how he talked with special care. It was another insight. On his pad he wrote the letter MK. The prisoner's diction and accent betrayed him. Mission Kaffir. Raised at one of the stations by foolish clergy as though he was one day going to be a white man. Of course, the word 'kaffir' was not a word in official use any longer. Like other names at that time growing less acceptable as descriptions of Africans: 'native', 'coon' and even 'Bantu', the word had given way to softer names in an attempt to respond to the disaffection springing up among black people. But du Preez, as he told himself, was too old a dog to learn new tricks. Besides, he was not interested in learning to be more 'responsive'. He did not belong to the ameliorists. His job was to control disaffection and where necessary to put it down with proper force. And anyway, his notes were strictly for his own reference, private reminders of his first impressions of a prisoner, useful when, and if, a second interview took place. The number of people he saw was growing daily and he could not expect to keep track of them all in his head.

Du Preez left his desk and slowly circled the prisoner. 'Your comrade who placed the bomb in the shopping-centre was a bungler. There was great damage. Many people were killed. Women and children among them. But he wasn't quick enough, your friend. The blast caught him too. Before he died he gave us your name. The paraffin tests show you handled explosives recently. I want the location of the cache. I want the make-up o your cell with names and addresses as well as anything else you might want to tell me.'

'If the bomb did its business then the man was no bungler,' Mpahlele said.

'The murder of women and children – no bungle?'

Mpahlele shrugged. 'Casualties of war.'

Du Preez circled him and stopped beside his right ear. 'I don't call the death of children war. I call it barbarism.'

'Our children have been dying for years but we have never called it barbarism. Now we are learning. You and I know what we mean. I'm your prisoner of war. You will do whatever you can to get me to tell you things you want to know. Then you will get rid of me. But I will tell you nothing. So why don't you finish with me now? Save time.' His brown eyes rested briefly and calmly on du Preez's empty chair, and then swept the room as if the man had said all he had to say and was now more interested in getting to know that notorious office.

A muscle in du Preez's cheek rippled and it took him a moment longer than he would have liked to bring his face back to a decent composure. Then he crossed to the big steel cabinet and opened it. Inside was the terrible, tangled paraphernalia of persuasion, the electric generator, the leads and electrodes, the salt water for sharpening contact and the thick leather straps necessary for restraining the shocked and writhing victim. At the sight of this he scored a point; he thought he detected a momentary pause, a faltering in the steady brown eyes taking stock of his office, and he pressed home the advantage. 'It's very seldom that people fail to talk to me after this treatment.' He held up the electrodes. 'The pain is intense.'

In fact, as we know now, the apparatus in the cabinet was not that actually used on prisoners – indeed, one can see the same equipment on permanent exhibition in the National Museum of the Revolution. Du Preez, in fact, kept it for effect. The real thing was administered by a special team in a soundproof room on one of the lower floors. But the mere sight of the equipment, whose reputation was huge among the townships and shanty towns, was often enough to have the effect of loosening stubborn tongues. However, Mpahlele looked at the tangle of wires and straps as if he wanted to include them in his inventory of the room and his expression suggested not fear but rather – and this du Preez found positively alarming – a hint of approval. There was nothing more to be said. He went back to his desk, pressed the buzzer and the plainclothes men came in and took Mpahlele downstairs.

Over the next twenty-four hours 'Window jumpin'' du Preez puzzled over his new prisoner. It was a long time before he put his finger on some of the qualities distinguishing this man from others he'd worked with under similar circumstances. Clearly, Mpahlele was not frightened. But then other men had been brave too – for a while. It was not only bravery, one had to add to it the strange fact that this man quite clearly did not hate him. That was quite alarming: Mpahlele had treated him as if they were truly equals. There was an effrontery about this he found maddening and the more he thought about it, the more he raged inside. He walked over to the windows behind his desk and gazed down to the dead little square with its empty benches and its crazy paving which, with its haphazard joins where the stones were cemented one to the next into nonsensical, snaking patterns, looked from the height of the thirteenth storey as if a giant had brought his foot down hard and the earth had shivered into a thousand pieces. He was getting angry. Worse, he was letting his anger cloud his judgment. Worse still, he didn't care.

Mpahlele was in a bad way when they brought him back to du Preez. His face was so bruised that the old knife scar was barely visible, his lower lip was bleeding copiously and he swayed when the policemen let him go and might have fallen had he not grabbed the edge of the desk and hung there swaying. In answer to du Preez's silent question the interrogators shook their heads. 'Nothing. He never said *nothing.*'

Mpahlele had travelled far in the regions of pain and it had changed him greatly. It might have been another man who clung to du Preez's desk with his breath coming in rusty pants: his throat was choked with phlegm or blood he did not have the strength to cough away. He was bent and old and clearly on his last legs. One eye was puffed up in a great swelling shot with green and purple bruises, but the other, he noticed with a renewed spurt of anger, though it had trouble focusing, showed the same old haughty gleam when he spoke to the man.

'Have you any more to tell me about your war?'

Mpahlele gathered himself with a great effort, his one good eye flickering wildly with the strain. He licked the blood off his lips and wiped it from his chin. 'We will win,' he said, 'soon.'

Du Preez dismissed the interrogators with a sharp nod and they left his presence by backing away to the door, full of awe at his control. When the door closed behind them he stood up and regarded the swaying figure with its flickering eye. 'You are like children,' he said bitterly, 'and there is nothing we can do for you.'

'Yes,' said Mpahlele, 'We are your children. We owe you everything.'

Du Preez stared at him. But there was not a trace of irony to be detected. The madman was quite plainly sincere in what he said and du Preez found that insufferable. He moved to the windows and opened them. It was now that, so the stories go, he made his fateful remark. 'Well, if you won't talk, then I suppose you had better learn to fly.'

What happened next is not clear except in broad outline even today, the records of the old regime which were to have been made public have unaccountably been reclassified as secret, but we can make an informed guess. Legend then says that du Preez recounted for his prisoner his 'theory of desperate solutions' and that, exhausted though he was, Mpahlele showed quickening interest in the way out chosen by white men – that is to say, dancing. We know this is true because du Preez told the policemen waiting outside the door when he joined them in order to allow Mpahlele to do what he had to do. After waiting a full minute, du Preez entered his office again closing the door behind him, alone, as had become customary in such cases, his colleagues respecting his need for a few moments of privacy before moving on to the next case. Seconds later these colleagues heard a most terrible cry. When they rushed into the room they found it was empty.

Now we are out on a limb. We have no more facts to go on. All is buried in obscurity or say, rather, it is buried with du Preez who plunged from his window down to the landing field at the most horrible speed, landing on his head. Jake Mpahlele has never spoken of his escape from Colonel 'Window jumpin'' du Preez. All we have are the stories. Some firmly believe to this day that it was done by a special magic and Mpahlele had actually learnt to fly and that the colonel on looking out of his window was so jealous at seeing a black man swooping in the heavens that he had plunged after him on the supposition, regarded as axiomatic in the days of the old regime, that anything a black man could do, a white man could do ten times better. Others, more sceptical, said that the prisoner had hidden himself in the steel cabinet with the torture equipment and emerged to push du Preez to hell and then escaped in the confusion you will get in a hive if you kill the queen bee. All that is known for sure is that du Preez lay on the landing field like wet clothes fallen from a washing-line, terribly twisted and leaking everywhere. And that in the early days of the new regime Jake Mpahlele was appointed chief investigating officer in charge of the interrogation of suspects and that his work with political prisoners, especially white prisoners, was soon so widely respected that he won rapid promotion to the rank of colonel and became known throughout the country as Colonel Jake 'Dancin'' Mpahlele, and after his name it was customary to add 'thank God', because he was a strong man and in the early days of the new regime everyone agreed we needed a strong man.

'Do You Love Me?'

Peter Carey

1 The Role of the Cartographers

Perhaps a few words about the role of the Cartographers in our present society are warranted.

To begin with one must understand the nature of the yearly census, a manifestation of our desire to know, always, exactly where we stand. The census, originally a count of the population, has gradually extended until it has become a total inventory of the contents of the nation, a mammoth task which is continuing all the time – no sooner has one census been announced than work on another begins.

The results of the census play an important part in our national life and have, for many years, been the pivot point for the yearly 'Festival of the Corn' (an ancient festival, related to the wealth of the earth).

We have a passion for lists. And nowhere is this more clearly illustrated than in the Festival of the Corn which takes place in midsummer, the weather always being fine and warm. On the night of the festival, the householders move their goods and possessions, all furniture, electrical goods, clothing, rugs, kitchen utensils, bathrobes, slippers, cushions, lawnmowers, curtains, doorstops, heirlooms, cameras, and anything else that can be moved into the street so that the census officials may the more easily check the inventory of each household.

The Festival of the Corn is, however, much more than a clerical affair. And, the day over and the night come, the householders invite each other to view their possessions which they refer to, on this night, as gifts. It is like nothing more than a wedding feast – there is much cooking, all sorts of traditional dishes, fine wines, strong liquors, music is played loudly in quiet neighbourhoods, strangers copulate with strangers, men dance together, and maidens in yellow robes distribute small barley sugar corncobs to young and old alike.

And in all this the role of the Cartographers is perhaps the most important, for our people crave, more than anything else, to know the extent of the nation, to know, exactly, the shape of the coastline, to hear what land may have been lost to the sea, to know what has been reclaimed and what is still in doubt. If the Cartographers' report is good the Festival of the Corn will be a good festival. If the report is bad, one can always sense, for all the dancing and drinking, a feeling of nervousness and apprehension in the revellers, a certain desperation. In the year of a bad Cartographers' report there will always be fights and, occasionally, some property will be stolen as citizens attempt to compensate themselves for their sense of loss.

Because of the importance of their job the Cartographers have become an elite – well-paid, admired, envied, and having no small opinion of themselves. It is said by some that they are over-proud, immoral, vain and foot-loose, and it is perhaps the last charge (by necessity true) that brings about the others. For the Cartographers spend their years travelling up and down the coast, along the great rivers, traversing great mountains and vast deserts. They travel in small parties of three, four, sometimes five, making their own time, working as they please, because eventually it is their own responsibility to see that their team's task is completed in time.

My father, a Cartographer himself, often told me stories about himself or his colleagues and the adventures they had in the wilderness.

There were other stories, however, that always remained in my mind and, as a child, caused me considerable anxiety. These were the stories of the nether regions and I doubt if they were known outside a very small circle of Cartographers and government officials. As a child in a house frequented by Cartographers, I often heard these tales which invariably made me cling closely to my mother's skirts.

It appears that for some time certain regions of the country had become less and less real and these regions were regarded fearfully even by the Cartographers, who prided themselves on their courage. The regions in question were invariably uninhabited, unused for agriculture or industry. There were certain sections of the Halverson Ranges, vast stretches of the Greater Desert, and long pieces of coastline which had begun to slowly disappear like the image on an improperly fixed photograph.

It was because of these nebulous areas that the Fischerscope was introduced. The Fischerscope is not unlike radar in its principle and is able to detect the presence of any object, no matter how dematerialized or insubstantial. In this way the Cartographers were still able to map the questionable parts of the nether regions. To have returned with blanks on the maps would have created such public anxiety that no one dared think what it might do to the stability of our society. I now have reason to believe that certain areas of the country disappeared so completely that even the Fischerscope could not detect them and the Cartographers, acting under political pressure, used old maps to fake-in the missing sections. If my theory is grounded in fact, and I am sure it is, it would explain my father's cynicism about the Festival of the Corn.

2 The Archetypal Cartographer

My father was in his fifties but he had kept himself in good shape. His skin was brown and his muscles still firm. He was a tall man with a thick head of grey hair, a slightly less grey moustache and a long aquiline nose. Sitting on a horse he looked as proud and cruel as Genghis Khan. Lying on the beach clad only in bathers and sunglasses he still managed to retain his authoritative air.

Beside him I always felt as if I had betrayed him. I was slightly built, more like my mother.

It was the day before the festival and we lay on the beach, my father, my mother, my girlfriend and I. As was usual in these circumstances my father addressed all his remarks to Karen. He never considered the members of his own family worth talking to. I always had the uncomfortable feeling that he was flirting with my girlfriends and I never knew what to do about it.

People were lying in groups up and down the beach. Near us a family of five were playing with a large beach ball.

'Look at those fools,' my father said to Karen.

'Why are they fools?' Karen asked.

'They're fools,' said my father. 'They were born fools and they'll die fools. Tomorrow they'll dance in the streets and drink too much.'

'So,' said Karen triumphantly, in the manner of one who has become privy to secret information. 'It will be a good Cartographers' report?'

My father roared with laughter.

Karen looked hurt and pouted. 'Am I a fool?'

'No,' my father said, 'you're really quite splendid.'

3 The Most Famous Festival

The festival, as it turned out, was the greatest disaster in living memory.

The Cartographers' report was excellent, the weather was fine, but somewhere something had gone wrong.

The news was confusing. The television said that, in spite of the good report, various items had been stolen very early in the night. Later there was a news flash to say that a large house had completely disappeared in Howie Street.

Later still we looked out the window to see a huge band of people carrying lighted torches. There was a lot of shouting. The same image, exactly, was on the television and a reporter was explaining that bands of vigilantes were out looking for thieves.

My father stood at the window, a martini in his hand, and watched the vigilantes set alight a house opposite.

My mother wanted to know what we should do.

'Come and watch the fools,' my father said, 'they're incredible.'

4 The I.C.I. Incident

The next day the I.C.I. building disappeared in front of a crowd of two thousand people. It took two hours. The crowd stood silently as the great steel and glass structure slowly faded before them.

The staff who were evacuated looked pale and shaken. The caretaker who was amongst the last to leave looked almost translucent. In the days that followed he made some name for himself as a mystic, claiming that he had been able to see other worlds, layer upon layer, through the fabric of the here and now.

5 Behaviour when Confronted with Dematerialization

The anger of our people when confronted with acts of theft has always been legendary and was certainly highlighted by the incidents which occurred on the night of the festival.

But the fury exhibited on this famous night could not compare with the intensity of emotion displayed by those who witnessed the earliest scenes of dematerialization.

The silent crowd who watched the I.C.I. building erupted into hysteria when they realized that it had finally gone and wasn't likely to come back.

It was like some monstrous theft for which punishment must be meted out.

They stormed into the Shell building next door and smashed desks and ripped down office partitions. Reporters who attended the scene were rarely impartial observers, but one of the cooler-headed members of the press remarked on the great number of weeping men and women who hurled typewriters from windows and scattered files through crowds of frightened office workers.

Five days later they displayed similar anger when the Shell building itself disappeared.

6 Behaviour of Those Dematerializing

The first reports of dematerializing people were not generally believed and were suppressed by the media. But these things were soon common knowledge and few families were untouched by them. Such incidents were obviously not all the same but in many victims there was a tendency to exhibit extreme aggression towards those around them. Murders and assaults committed by these unfortunates were not uncommon and in most cases they exhibited an almost unbelievable rage, as if they were the victims of a shocking betrayal.

My friend James Bray was once stopped in the street by a very beautiful woman who clawed and scratched at his face and said: 'You did this to me you bastard, you did this to me.'

He had never seen her before but he confessed that, in some irrational way, he felt responsible and didn't defend himself. Fortunately she disappeared before she could do him much damage.

7 Some Theories that Arose at the Time

1 The world is merely a dream dreamt by god who is waking after a long sleep. When he is properly awake the world will disappear completely. When the world disappears we will disappear with it and be happy.

2 The world has become sensitive to light. In the same way that prolonged use of say penicillin can suddenly result in a dangerous allergy, prolonged exposure of the world to the sun has made it sensitive to light.

The advocates of this theory could be seen bustling through the city crowds in their long, hooded black robes.

3 The fact that the world is disappearing has been caused by the sloppy work of the Cartographers and census-takers. Those who filled out their census forms incorrectly would lose those items they had neglected to describe. People overlooked in the census by impatient officials would also disappear. A strong pressure

group demanded that a new census be taken quickly before matters got worse.

8 My Father's Theory

The world, according to my father, was exactly like the human body and had its own defence mechanisms with which it defended itself against anything that either threatened it or was unnecessary to it. The I.C.I. building and the I.C.I. company had obviously constituted some threat to the world or had simply been irrelevant. That's why it had disappeared and not because some damn fool god was waking up and rubbing his eyes.

'I don't believe in god,' my father said. 'Humanity is god. Humanity is the only god I know. If humanity doesn't need something it will disappear. People who are not loved will disappear. Everything that is not loved will disappear from the face of the earth. We only exist through the love of others and that's what it's all about.'

9 A Contradiction

'Look at those fools,' my father said, 'they wouldn't know if they were up themselves.'

10 An Unpleasant Scene

The world at this time was full of unpleasant and disturbing scenes. One that I recall vividly took place in the middle of the city on a hot, sultry Tuesday afternoon. It was about one-thirty and I was waiting for Karen by the post office when a man of forty or so ran past me. He was dematerializing rapidly. Everybody seemed to be deliberately looking the other way, which seemed to me to make him dematerialize faster. I stared at him hard, hoping that I could do something to keep him there until help arrived. I tried to love him, because I believed in my father's theory. I thought, I must love that man. But his face irritated me. It is not so easy to love a stranger and I'm ashamed to say that he had the small mouth and close-together eyes that I have always disliked in a person. I tried to love him but I'm afraid I failed.

While I watched he tried to hail taxi after taxi. But the taxi drivers were only too well aware of what was happening and had no wish to spend their time driving a passenger who, at any moment, might cease to exist. They looked the other way or put up their NOT FOR HIRE signs.

Finally he managed to waylay a taxi at some traffic-lights. By this time he was so insubstantial that I could see right through him. He was beginning to shout. A terrible thin noise, but penetrating none the less. He tried to open the cab door, but the driver had already locked it. I could hear the man's voice, high and piercing: 'I want to go home.' He repeated it over and over again. 'I want to go home to my wife.'

The taxi drove off when the lights changed. There was a lull in the traffic. People had fled the corner and left it deserted and it was I alone who saw the man finally disappear.

I felt sick.

Karen arrived five minutes later and found me pale and shaken. 'Are you all right?' she said.

'Do you love me?' I said.

11 The Nether Regions

My father had an irritating way of explaining things to me I already understood, refusing to stop no matter how much I said 'I know' or 'You told me before.'

Thus he expounded on the significance of the nether regions, adopting the tone of a lecturer speaking to a class of particularly backward children.

'As you know,' he said, 'the nether regions were amongst the first to disappear and this in itself is significant. These regions, I'm sure you know, are seldom visited by men and only then by

157

people like me whose sole job is to make sure that they're still there. We had no use for these areas, these deserts, swamps, and coastlines which is why, of course, they disappeared. They were merely possessions of ours and if they had any use at all it was as symbols for our poets, writers and film-makers. They were used as symbols of alienation, lovelessness, loneliness, uselessness and so on. Do you get what I mean?'

'Yes,' I said, 'I get what you mean.'

'But do you?' My father insisted. 'But do you really, I wonder.' He examined me seriously, musing on the possibilities of my understanding him. 'How old are you?'

'Twenty,' I said.

'I knew, of course,' he said. 'Do you understand the significance of the nether regions?'

I sighed, a little too loudly and my father narrowed his eyes. Quickly I said: 'They are like everything else. They're like the cities. The cities are deserts where people are alone and lonely. They don't love one another.'

'Don't love one another,' intoned my father, also sighing. 'We no longer love one another. When we realize that we need one another we will stop disappearing. This is a lesson to us. A hard lesson, but, I hope, an effective one.'

My father continued to speak, but I watched him without listening. After a few minutes he stopped abruptly: 'Are you listening to me?' he said. I was surprised to detect real concern in his voice. He looked at me questioningly. 'I've always looked after you,' he said, 'ever since you were little.'

12 The Cartographers' Fall

I don't know when it was that I noticed that my father had become depressed. It probably happened quite gradually without either my mother or me noticing it.

Even when I did become aware of it I attributed it to a woman. My father had a number of lovers and his moods usually reflected the success or failure of these relationships.

But I know now that he had heard already of Hurst and Jamov, the first two Cartographers to disappear. The news was suppressed for several weeks and then, somehow or other, leaked to the press. Certainly the Cartographers had enemies amongst the civil servants who regarded them as over-proud and overpaid, and it was probably from one of these civil servants that the press heard the news.

When the news finally broke I understood my father's depression and felt sorry for him.

I didn't know how to help him. I wanted, badly, to make him happy. I had never ever been able to give him anything or do anything for him that he couldn't do better himself. Now I wanted to help him, to show him I understood.

I found him sitting in front of the television one night when I returned from my office and I sat quietly beside him. He seemed more kindly now and he placed his hand on my knee and patted it.

I sat there for a while, overcome with the new warmth of this relationship and then, unable to contain my emotion any more, I blurted out: 'You could change your job.'

My father stiffened and sat bolt upright. The pressure of his hand on my knee increased until I yelped with pain, and still he held on, hurting me terribly.

'You are a fool,' he said, 'you wouldn't know if you were up yourself.'

Through the pain in my leg, I felt the intensity of my father's fear.

13 Why the World Needs Cartographers

My father woke me at 3 a.m. to tell me why the world needed Cartographers. He smelled of whisky and seemed, once again, to be very gentle.

'The world needs Cartographers,' he said softly, 'because if they didn't have Cartographers the fools wouldn't know where they were. They wouldn't know if they were up themselves if they didn't have a Cartographer to tell them what's happening. The world needs Cartographers,' my father said, 'it needs Cartographers.'

14 One Final Scene

Let me describe a final scene to you: I am sitting on the sofa my father brought home when I was five years old. I am watching television. My father is sitting in a leather armchair that once belonged to his father and which has always been exclusively his. My mother is sitting in the dining alcove with her cards spread across the table, playing one more interminable game of patience.

I glance casually across at my father to see if he is doing anything more than stare into space, and notice, with a terrible shock, that he is showing the first signs of dematerializing.

'What are you staring at?' My father, in fact, has been staring at me.

'Nothing.'

'Well, don't.'

Nervously I return my eyes to the inanity of the television. I don't know what to do. Should I tell my father that he is dematerializing? If I don't tell him will he notice? I feel I should do something but I can feel, already, the anger in his voice. His anger is nothing new. But this is possibly the beginning of a tide of uncontrollable rage. If he knows he is dematerializing, he will think I don't love him. He will blame me. He will attack me. Old as he is, he is still considerably stronger than I am and he could hurt me badly. I stare determinedly at the television and feel my father's eyes on me.

I try to feel love for my father, I try very, very hard.

I attempt to remember how I felt about him when I was little, in the days when he was still occasionally tender towards me.

But it's no good.

Because I can only remember how he has hit me, hurt me, humiliated me and flirted with my girlfriends. I realize, with a

160

flush of panic and guilt, that I don't love him. In spite of which I say: 'I love you.'

My mother looks up sharply from her cards and lets out a surprised cry.

I turn to my father. He has almost disappeared. I can see the leather of the chair through his stomach.

I don't know whether it is my unconvincing declaration of love or my mother's exclamation that makes my father laugh. For whatever reason, he begins to laugh uncontrollably: 'You bloody fools,' he gasps, 'I wish you could see the looks on your bloody silly faces.'

And then he is gone.

My mother looks across at me nervously, a card still in her hand. 'Do you love me?' she asks.

Commentary

Revenge *Ellen Gilchrist*

Ellen Gilchrist grew up in the 'deep South' of America, in the Mississippi Delta – the setting for much of her fiction to date. She has published one novel, *The Annunciation* (Faber & Faber, 1984), and three wonderfully entertaining collections of interlinked stories: *In the Land of Dreamy Dreams* (Faber & Faber, 1981; Pavane, 1987), *Victory Over Japan* (Faber & Faber, 1984), and *Drunk with Love* (Faber & Faber, 1987). Within each volume, the stories are clustered, and the same characters recur across a range of stories. Rhoda Manning, for example, the girl in *Revenge*, appears in all three books, at different points in her always eventful life. Like so many of Gilchrist's female characters, Rhoda is driven in these stories by a reckless energy, a supreme self-confidence, that brings her into regular conflict with those of more conventional behaviour. At the same time, for all their excesses, the characters and events in Gilchrist's stories are always very easy to imagine. *Revenge* is taken from *In the Land of Dreamy Dreams*.

Ideas for discussion

Rhoda, from Indiana, spends the summer of 1944 at her grandmother's big house in the deep South, while her father is with the American army in Europe. Her five male cousins are soon in preparation for the resumption of the Olympic Games. What is Rhoda's grandmother's idea (shared by Miss Onnie Maud) of how a little girl should behave, and what she should grow up to be?

Rhoda herself has other ideas. (*It's the movies*, says Miss Onnie Maud, *they let her watch anything she likes in Indiana*.) What attracts Rhoda to the company of Baby Doll, and especially Lauralee Manning? What does she admire in Lauralee, who *seemed so splendid* (p. 8)?

Living in the southern states of America during the Second W.
War, Rhoda has picked up a particular vocabulary of racial abuse. Wr.
is the effect on the household (and on the reader) when she calls the
family friend, for example, a *goddamned nigger German spy* (p. 3)?

How do her male cousins see her? (Are they at all justified in this?)
How must she appear to the shop assistants in Nell's and Blum's? To
Baby Doll? To Donald Marcus, who *had never seen anything like it in his
whole life* (p. 12)? Would you like her as your sister?

Re-read the half page or so beginning *At night they pulled their cots
together . . .* (p. 4). What is it that makes the voice of this narrator so
entertaining? Does she sound like a ten-year-old?

What is the attraction to Rhoda of being a Maid of Honor? And why,
in the event, is it not enough? Do you like the ending?

Ideas for writing

☐ Write a character study of Rhoda, using the evidence of the text.

☐ Or achieve the same end by inviting four or five of the other
characters in the story to contribute a paragraph of reminiscences about
'*the summer of the Broad Jump Pit*'. You could begin by tape-recording
their contributions.

☐ Take the episode in Nell's and Blum's Department Store (pp. 10–
11), and re-write it in the form of a stage or TV script. Include the
conversations between the sales ladies that go on outside the dressing-
room, and the remarks made in Rhoda's presence which she does not
hear.

Girl   *Jamaica Kincaid*

Jamaica Kincaid was born in St John's, Antigua, in the West Indies.
She now lives in New York, where she works as a journalist. *At the
Bottom of the River* (Picador, 1984), from which this story is taken, was
her first book, a richly poetic collection of meditative, often dream-like,
fictions. She has also published a novel, *Annie John* (Picador, 1988).

Ideas for discussion

It is clear that this piece is written to be spoken, but it is not in a
'naturalistic' spoken form – no one gives quite that much advice in a
single mouthful. Is this a single voice, or a mixture of voices? How
might it be read aloud? Working in small groups, prepare a reading of
Girl.

What is the effect of putting together in a single sentence such a .oriously random assortment of folk-wisdom and parental instruction? What does it tell us about the world into which the girl is being 'socialised', or taught to fit in?

How do males feature in this world? How is the girl to treat them?

What is the girl's implied mood, for instance, in the two words she manages to slip in edgeways? Is she bitter? Resigned? Accepting? How much laughter is there in this writing?

Ideas for writing

☐ What behaviour is expected of the girl? How is it different from the behaviour which might be expected of a boy?

☐ Think of the voices that aim to 'socialise' you, at home and/or at school, into a particular way of thinking or behaving, and write a similar piece.

Sweet Sixteen   *Michelene Wandor*

Michelene Wandor, born in London in 1940, has worked as a poetry editor and theatre reviewer for *Time Out* magazine, and has written extensively for theatre and radio. Her publications include a volume of plays, two books of poetry, and an intriguing collection of what the author prefers to call fictions, entitled *Guests in the Body* (Virago 1986). In this collection, the theme of 'possession' is explored in a variety of contexts and fictional forms.

Ideas for discussion

On the surface of it, rearranging the supermarket shelves ought not to provoke the kind of panic it does here. Why is the change in weekly routine so alarming? Is the women's behaviour rational? Does the writer persuade you to believe in it? (Even before the final outburst, it seems to me that the language is flickering with dangerous possibilities – *The frozen, sleeping raspberries*, for example.)

There is clearly a strong element of fantasy in the story's climax. Have you yourself ever wanted to behave like this – particularly in supermarkets? Is the fantasy satisfying? Do you recognise the kind of language in which the food is described in the paragraph beginning *The women look at each other . . .* (p. 20)?

Until the police arrive, the world of the story is entirely fer. Could you imagine a male version, or is the story about a specific female experience?

At either end of the story, and separated from it, is an image taken from the *soft-focus* commercial in the window of the adjacent TV rental shop. Why is the image introduced in this way? How does it relate to the main narrative? (What is the effect of watching sixteen televisions together?)

Ideas for writing

□ Write the official report of the police sergeant (male) who was the first to arrive on the scene.

□ Imagine the interview in the manager's office, or at the police-station, where Naomi is questioned about her behaviour.

□ Write a short story which explores in some way the gap between the language and images of TV commercials, and the language and images of everyday reality.

Queen for a Day   *Russell Banks*

Russell Banks was born in New England, USA, and has lived and worked in both the USA and the Caribbean. He now teaches at Princeton University, New York. He has published a number of novels in America, though his work is less widely known in Britain, where the publication of *Continental Drift* (Hamish Hamilton, 1985; Penguin, 1986), a complex and harrowing novel of contemporary American life, has been followed by the collection *Success Stories* (Hamish Hamilton, 1986), from which *Queen for a Day* is taken. Like Ellen Gilchrist, Russell Banks devotes a number of the stories in this collection to episodes in the life of a single character, Earl Painter, growing up during the 1950s in small-town industrial America.

Ideas for discussion

Few writers have convinced me as strongly as does Russell Banks of the *truthfulness* of what he writes about. From the initial scene in the boys' bedroom, through to the final phone-call, the sense for me is of a devastating authenticity. How does the writer achieve this sense of truth to life? What might be said, for example, about the dialogue in the y, about the use of the present tense, about how the writer manages convey Earl's inner feelings?

When the father leaves, Earl *knew that in many ways it was the best their father could do for them and in many other ways it was the worst* (p. 26). He is forced into the adult world of *obscure needs and desires* (p. 40), and of difficult choices, a world into which the reader must follow him. He hangs on to an ideal of family life (see for instance the paragraph starting *It's dark . . .* on p. 38) but cannot bring himself to forgive the father's treatment of the family, his continual betrayal. In this dilemma, there is no one – apart from Jack Bailey – to whom he can turn.

What is your opinion of the TV show *Queen for a Day*, in which the audience's compassion is measured by a clapometer, and the suffering of successful contestants rewarded with glamorous prizes? What elements in the show appealed to its viewers, do you think? Would such a show prove popular on TV today? Does it bear any resemblance to any of our own write-in or game-shows?

Re-read the episode beginning *At the sound of the front door . . .* (p. 33–5), in which the mother returns home after being sacked from the Tannery. What strikes you about the dialogue which Earl overhears? About the way Earl behaves throughout this scene? About the way Adele Painter responds to Earl's behaviour?

For the Catholic priest, Father LaCoy, there is a straightforward moral solution to the family's difficulties: divorce is forbidden by the church, therefore the parents should get back together. Does this satisfy you as a solution?

The climax of the story is the phone-call between Earl and his father, in which all kinds of emotions come successively to the surface. A prepared reading aloud may be helpful. How, for example, does Earl say: *Sure. Why not? Try* (p. 46), and how does the father react? Are you convinced by the father's repentance – does he indeed *deserve a second chance*? At what point does Earl weaken? Does Earl want his father back? (How does he say *Daddy, are you gonna try to get back together with Mom?* (p. 47)) Is Earl right to take the responsibility, which he appears to have done, for turning his father away?

Is the ending conclusive?

Ideas for writing

☐ Write a letter from Adele Painter to Nelson Painter, in which she describes how things have been, and suggests either a reconciliation or a divorce. Choose the date of the letter carefully, and relate what she says to events in the story. If you wish, write Nelson's reply.

□ In a TV Company office, the producer's assistants are going through a pile of letters to *Queen for a Day*, including one of Earl's. Write the conversation.

Kid in a Bin   *Robert Carter*

The Australian writer Robert Carter was born in 1945. He has so far published a novel, *The Sugar Factory*, and a fiercely imaginative collection of stories, *The Pleasure Within* (Angus and Robertson, 1987), from which *Kid is a Bin* is taken.

Ideas for discussion

The opening paragraph of this story is not easily forgotten. Would it be possible for a child to live in this way? Is it imaginable?

One of the things that persuades me to believe in the story is the particular tone in which it is written. How would you describe the way the story is told? How involved did you become in Anthony's situation? As with a number of other stories in this collection, the present tense is used throughout. What is the effect of this?

There is a vividly comic side to Anthony's situation – the rubbish-bin's-eye-view of McDonalds, for example. What details in the story did you find amusing? In the final pages, the comedy evaporates. Skin cancer caused by exposure to the sun is an increasingly common cause of premature death, not least in Australia. The newspaper cuttings which the child possesses in the story could well have been reports of an actual case. Does this add up to a believable explanation for Anthony's behaviour?

In the final paragraph of the story, we return to the situation at the beginning. What kind of ending, and what kind of feelings, does this leave you with?

Ideas for writing

□ Re-trace your response to this story through a reading-log, noting your reactions as the story developed, and the details which particularly captured your attention.

□ In one sense, the story still lacks an ending – there are several points where Anthony is almost found out, and it is clear that the situation cannot continue indefinitely. Write the scene in which Anthony is discovered.

No Longer the Warehouseman   *James Kelman*

James Kelman was born in Glasgow in 1946. He left school at fifteen for a trade apprenticeship, and has since worked in a variety of jobs, with periods of unemployment. His novels and stories have focused unblinkingly upon the day-to-day experience of the urban poor in contemporary Scotland; it is a bleakly uncompromising, though often humorous, vision. The stories are for the most part extremely short, and rarely conventional; the monologue, as here, is a characteristic form. James Kelman's stories are collected in *Not, Not While the Giro and other stories* (Polygon, 1983), from which the present story is taken; in *Greyhound for Breakfast* (Secker and Warburg, 1987; Picador, 1988); and in *Lean Tales* (Penguin, 1987), which also contains stories by fellow Scots Agnes Owens and Alasdair Gray.

Ideas for discussion

One of the things that interests me about Kelman as a writer is his knack of writing voices down, of getting inside the heads of characters. The very awkwardness of the writing, as in the present example, forces the reader to attend more closely to the language used, and from this brief monologue, or speech for a single voice, we can establish a good deal about the narrator's past history and current state of mind. Try reading parts of it aloud. How fluent and rhythmical is this writing? How composed? How confident? What kinds of job has the man done in the past? What is suggested by his vocabulary and turn of phrase?

I was of course cool, polite . . . (p. 58) *. . . one feels there is something wrong with one . .* (p. 58) . . . Do you get any sense of how the long period of unemployment has affected the narrator? In his relationship with others, for example?

My wife is to be forgiven if she . . . what. (p. 59) Is there any significance in what the speaker chooses *not* to say?

How realistic is this man about his own situation? What is his attitude towards social security? Listening to the man's voice, do you blame him or pity him for what happens? Is he a sad or a comic figure? (Can he be both?)

Ideas for writing

Given the self-absorption of the narrator, it might be interesting to explore how other characters see him.

□ Write a scene in which one of the other warehousemen entertains a friend with his version of the story of the new employee.

□ Or tell the story from the point of view of the narrator's wife. What has she lived through this past year? What thoughts go through her mind during her husband's first day back at work? What are her reactions when he returns home?

□ Using this story as an example, write a monologue of your own in which the voice of the speaker clearly establishes his or her character, as well as telling the events of the story.

White Places   *Mary Flanagan*

Mary Flanagan was born in New Hampshire, USA, and emigrated to England in 1969. She started writing at the age of thirty-six, and published her first collection of stories, the sharply entertaining *Bad Girls*, in 1984 (Macdonald/Futura, 1985). She has since published a novel, *Trust* (Penguin, 1988).

Ideas for discussion

How unusual is the behaviour of the children in this story? Is there anything which is reminiscent of your own childhood, or of children you know? What is your attitude towards the cruelty of Cissie and Celeste? What is it we enjoy about the story?

What impression does the story give us of the two sets of parents involved – Mr and Mrs Doyle, who have the girls at Easter, and Aunt Lillian and Uncle Raymond, who have them at Christmas? Do they know what goes on? Are they good parents?

Why does Charlotte/Killer become a victim? Is it to do with her own nature, or that of the others? What do you make of Killer's sense that *They needed less love than she did* (p. 68)?

One central difference between Killer and the other children is their attitude to Pretends: *She saw how much it thrilled them to make believe ... Why did they want to be something they weren't?* (p. 64) With which attitude do you most sympathise here?

When Killer is imprisoned in the snow fort, she believes that she is being punished, perhaps by God, for the crimes she – as Elvira – had committed. *Her crime had been so terrible* ... (p. 68). Do the other children also confuse Pretend and reality in this way?

Why, in the end, does Killer choose June?

Ideas for writing

□ Write about the first Pretend that the girls play after Killer has recovered. Keep in mind what you know of the children's characters, and what you think they may have learned from the affair of the snow fort. Write in story or script form.

□ Imagine yourself as one of the children grown up, reminiscing with a friend about those childhood vacations, and in particular about the snow fort. What do you think about it all now, as an adult?

The Werewolf *Angela Carter*

Angela Carter was born in England in 1940, and is the author of a dozen stylish and highly imaginative works of fiction, including *Nights at the Circus* (Chatto & Windus, 1984; Picador, 1986), and three volumes of short stories. She is a writer for whom myth, fantasy and fairy tale are fertile ground (she has translated the fairy tales of Charles Perrault). She has also shown a consistent preoccupation with gender and sexuality. *The Bloody Chamber* (Gollancz, 1979), from which *The Werewolf* is taken, is a collection of rewritten fairy tales; Angela Carter's most recent book of short fiction, *Black Venus* (Chatto & Windus, 1985; Picador, 1986) shows the same pleasure in re-working legend and history.

Ideas for discussion

At the heart of this story is a well-known fairy-tale, and it may be as well to begin by piecing together the version of the story that you yourself remember, and if possible comparing it with that of others. Are there any discrepancies?

In its traditional form, what does this tale say to children? Is it a cautionary, or moral tale, intended to warn children against bad behaviour? Is it simply an infant spine-chiller?

How does Angela Carter's version differ from the version you remember? Are there any particular moments of surprise or confusion? Who is missing from this version altogether? Is the story told in a different style?

Before beginning the narrative proper, the writer sketches for us a world in which superstitions about witches and werewolves are known to have been held: the story is in this way placed in a context that helps to interpret it – it becomes a different sort of story. What does *this* version of the story say to its hearers?

Ideas for writing

□ Find any version of *Red Riding Hood*, and show in what ways *The Werewolf* resembles it, and in what ways it differs. Consider both the sequence of events, and the manner in which the stories are told.

□ There is a strong similarity between the unusual goings-on of the typical fairy tale, and the kind of sensational human interest stories which make for juicy headlines in the popular press: *Virgin Lived With Seven Midgets, Court Told*, as Adrian Mitchell has it somewhere. How would the popular press report the story of Red Riding Hood – or any other well-known fairy-tale?

□ *The Bloody Chamber* also contains another version of Red Riding Hood – *The Company of Wolves* – and reinterpretations of Puss-in-Boots, Beauty and the Beast, and The Sleeping Beauty. Angela Carter is by no means the only writer to have rewritten old tales for a serious contemporary purpose. Try rewriting an old tale in this way.

A Tally of the Souls of Sheep   *Keri Hulme*

Keri Hulme is a New Zealander, of Maori, Scots and English ancestry. Her first novel, *The Bone People* (Hodder & Stoughton, 1985), won the Pegasus Prize for Maori Literature and the Booker Prize for Fiction. The bilingual title of her second book, *The Windeater/Te Kaihau* (Hodder & Stoughton, 1987), indicates the extent of Keri Hulme's immersion in Maori culture. The stories in *The Windeater* are characterised by an impassioned respect for the mysterious lives of creatures, and the sense of a lost relationship with the natural world. The book is notable also for the author's willingness to experiment with the forms a story can take, and *A Tally of the Souls of Sheep* is one example of this.

171

Ideas for discussion

A Tally of the Souls of Sheep is a deliberate brain-teaser. As much as any piece in this collection, it needs talking through with other readers.

In reading the story, you will need to draw upon your experience as a viewer – or reader – of narrative films. The story is presented in the form of a film-script, or storyboard, with sound-effects and other directions in a parallel column. There is a sense in which any story invites its readers to make a film in their heads; this one specifically asks its readers to do so – *How's your mind's eye?* asks Keri Hulme at one point.

The story also calls upon a variety of cinematic techniques – the implications of certain kinds of cut, for example, or the effect of a sound track which does not always correspond directly to what is seen. Do you recognise the genre, or type of film, in Keri Hulme's mind? What broad category of film types would you put it into, and which moments in the story lead you to decide this? (Do the members of the family realise what kind of film they are in?)

The script attends closely to shots and effects (or FX, as film-scripts term them) both audio and visual. The mind's eye of the reader is instructed to track, pan and zoom, is *airborne* in Action 16, *handheld* in Action 3. (In Action 20, the camera itself appears – what is the effect of that?) If you are unfamiliar with the technical language of filming, LS = Long Shot, CU = Close-up, MCU = Medium Close-up.

The Man is a freezing worker – that is, he works in a slaughterhouse where New Zealand Lamb is frozen for export: one way and another, meat features significantly in the story. At times, what we see or hear in the film is at least partly occurring in the man's head. How would you interpret the montage in Action 1 (a montage is a series of connected images, either run rapidly together or superimposed upon one another – in this case as part of a split screen)?

What is the effect of the CU on the man's eyes in Actions 1, 6 and 13? In film language, what does this tell us? (And what, therefore, is the significance of the CU on the woman's face in Action 13?)

The man's image is also accompanied at three points by a Phantom Voice – not his own voice, but *coming from the man's head* (p. 75). This Voice speaks in fragments of poetry, perhaps of a single poem. What is the poem about? Who or what does the Voice represent?

How is the Woman different from the Man, in the way they are presented, and in their reactions to events?

In contrast to the holidaying family, how is the natural world – landscape, sea, wild creatures – presented in the story? The initial description of Kaitangata Bay, for example? How do the birds and the sheep feature in the action? What is the effect of a line like *The woman is cooking rib-bones and breast muscles* (p. 84)?

The five *possible endings* all seem to be variations on a type: each gives us a little more to go on but none tells the whole story. Which ending would have the most dramatic impact? Which comes closest to offering an explanation of what has happened? Whichever ending is chosen, there is also the option of adding the *Finale* What would be the effect of that?

The story's title bears thinking about. The assumption that sheep have souls is in itself suggestive. (Also, the inclusion of birds and animals in the list of Characters.) Keri Hulme suggests various possible meanings of *tally*. The most helpful seem to me to be those which suggest a counting up, a reckoning, a holding to account . . . What does the title mean to you?

Ideas for writing

□ Trace the character of the Woman from her initial appearance, through her reactions to the holiday cottage, and to subsequent events. Can you suggest what the woman represents?

□ Is the film/story intended simply to entertain (by frightening) the reader/viewer, or does it invite us to think further? What interpretation would you offer?

□ Take any story in this collection and make a film of it, or of part of it, using the form of *A Tally of the Souls of Sheep*, and perhaps some of the techniques of film-making discussed above. You may wish to reorganise the order of events, and to leave out some of the dialogue or descriptive detail, but try to stay close to the heart of the original story. And try not to use a Narrator to fill in the tricky bits – devise some other means!

The Drover's Wife   *Murray Bail*

Murray Bail was born in Adelaide, Australia, in 1941. He has lived in Bombay, London and Sydney, working as a journalist and in advertising. A collection of short fictions, *Contemporary Portraits*, was published in Australia in 1975, and republished in Britain under the title *The Drover's Wife* (Faber & Faber) in 1986. It is a playful, cunningly written volume, full of the kind of comic invention that ıngers unsettlingly in the mind. A novel, *Homesickness*, appeared in 1980.

Ideas for discussion

Thirty years after his wife left him, a man is convinced that he has come across her portrait in a book of reproductions, painted shortly after she disappeared. Poring over the picture through a magnifying glass, Gordon evaluates the evidence, and gives us his version of events.

Listen to Gordon's voice as he reports his findings. What kind of voice is it? (Is he talking, or writing?) How would you describe his character? Is he mad?

Gordon never doubts that he has correctly identified his wife in the picture. He is equally certain about the correctness of *his* version of their marriage. What was it that he found so off-putting about Hazel's behaviour and appearance? Is there a pattern to it? What does he mean by her *silly streak*, for instance? How might others describe it?

Why should this man be so uncomfortable in the outback, in what he calls *the rotten landscape*? Why has he had such little success with human relationships? Is he a purely comic figure, or is there a note of sadness here?

Ideas for writing

□ Using the evidence of the story, recreate the picture which Gordon has seen, either by using your own words to describe it, or by drawing or painting it.

□ *The Drover's Wife* is Gordon's version of a marriage, and the author makes it clear how one-sided that version is. Write Hazel's version, including the same anecdotes – the snowballing scene, the camping holiday – but retold from *her* point of view.

□ Paintings are often a fruitful starting-point for poems or stories. What Murray Bail does, in addition, is to invent the writer of the story. Take any picture that intrigues you, decide who you are in relation to it, and write the story that lies behind it, finding a voice to match the character you have assumed.

Tree   *Neil Jordan*

Neil Jordan was born in Sligo, in Eire, in 1950. *Night in Tunisia*

174

(Dublin, 1976; Chatto & Windus, 1983), the collection of stories from which *Tree* is taken, was a remarkably accomplished first book. He has since written two novels, including *The Dream of a Beast* (Chatto & Windus, 1983), and written and directed a number of films including *The Company of Wolves* based on the Angela Carter story mentioned earlier, and co-scripted with her.

Ideas for discussion

I find this a haunting story – not easy, but well worth exploring carefully.

A couple are on a touring holiday in Ireland, visiting an area rich in history and superstition, where legends of St Brigid still persist. We know little of who they are, except that the man has a disabled leg, and their relationship has reached the point where they find it difficult at times to speak without contradicting each other. Despite all the *talking out* they have done in the past, their feelings are still submerged, obscure both to themselves and to each other: they, like the reader, are *groping towards a meaning* (p. 101).

The sight of the whitethorn tree catches the woman unawares. What does the flowering whitethorn mean to her personally? And why, when they drive on again, is she thinking of the man, John?

In the pub, she remembers *suddenly, vitally* the taste of whiskey, *gold, and volatile, filling not the tongue but the whole mouth* (p. 101). Why does she then say 'Whitethorn'? When they are leaving the pub, can you explain why they are angry with each other? Is it possible to square the man's *sadistic obscenities*, or the *awful blare* of the car horn, with the words *'I love you'*? What does she feel for him at this moment?

For the woman, both the whiskey and the whitethorn have acted as symbols – standing in her mind for something more than themselves. When she finally reaches the tree, its impossibility is explained. Do you see the tree as a fake, or a miracle? What does it now stand for? What is the mood of the ending?

Ideas for writing

☐ Explain the developing significance of the whitethorn tree for the woman in this story, from the first sighting, through to the final close encounter.

☐ Write another page or so to this story, in which the woman returns to the car.

☐ The crux of this relationship is to be found in the exchange on

. 102: *'I love you,' he said. 'I'm leaving,' she said.* Write a different story which also explores the complexity of people's feelings, and in which the same words are spoken.

Significant Moments in the Life of my Mother
Margaret Atwood

Margaret Atwood was born in Ottawa, Canada, in 1939, and grew up in the bush country of Northern Ontario. She is the author of more than twenty books, of poetry, fiction, and non-fiction, including two fine collections of stories – *Dancing Girls* (Jonathan Cape, 1982; Virago, 1984) and *Bluebeard's Egg* (Jonathan Cape, 1987; Virago 1988), from which the present story is taken. The subtle exploration of female experience, both private and social, is at the centre of Margaret Atwood's work. Her most recent novel, *The Handmaid's Tale* (Jonathan Cape, 1986; Virago, 1987) is a work of great power, a vision of the future in which the lives of women are regulated by an authoritarian and fundamentalist regime.

Ideas for discussion

In this story, the writer seems to be doing a number of things. She is piecing together a biography of her mother, made from the significant moments of her mother's favourite anecdotes, preserving and ordering her memories in the way one might preserve and order photographs in a family album. At the same time, she is reflecting upon her own childhood – or her mother's vision of it – in relation to the woman she herself has become. And she is also reflecting, both as a daughter and as a writer, upon the nature and function of these anecdotes: the very first story, the one about the Easter chicks, raises the question of *why* the story should be retold in quite this way.

Significant Moments spans the mother's lifetime, from her childhood as the daughter of a country doctor in Nova Scotia in the days before cars through her teenage years in the Twenties, marriage to a government official, and the birth of the writer and her brother; and finally to the birth of the writer's own daughter. *Now we are on more dangerous ground*, says the writer of the anecdotes in which she herself features: why should that be? And why is it that as the writer grew older, the mother appeared to have *few stories to tell about these times* (p. 119)? (The organisation of the stories is not entirely chronological:

the story of the mother's haircut, for example, recalls the story of the writer's own.) There seems to be no reason to doubt the biographical authenticity of these anecdotes: neither the mother nor the narrator, in that sense, is an invention. Does it therefore qualify as a story at all?

The writer is, first, a listener, a writer-down of the stories told by another. In doing so, she comes to understand more of a world significantly different from her own. What differences does she notice – in the behaviour of young people, for example? And as she scrutinises her own childhood, what evidence does she find of her own early conditioning, especially as a girl?

Male/female roles, across the generations, are a consistent point of interest for the writer. *Boys are great jokers . . . always up to something* (p. 110); women are to be protected from bad language, men from emotional pain (p. 113), and so on. It is interesting that the mother's father (the doctor) looms larger in these stories than the mother's husband (the civil servant): perhaps the anecdotes themselves have made him into more of a character. How is the writer's brother presented in these stories?

Stories in which members of the family *almost died* (p. 114), notes the writer, are relatively common; as is the sense of *sustained hilarity* (p. 108). Why should this be so? Why are some stories told *to women only, usually in the kitchen . . . in a lowered voice . . .* (p. 113)? When telling the story of the hammered thumb, the mother's eyes *shine with delight* (p. 112); *this story*, says the writer, *illustrates several things . . .*; or, later, *This may be the real point of the story . . .* (p. 115). Does Margaret Atwood help you to understand some of the reasons *why* people make stories of their lives?

Ideas for writing

□ What have you understood from this story about the relationship, over time, between the writer and her mother?

□ To a younger generation, the repetitiveness of the stories told by older relatives can often appear tedious; but later, when the old folk stop talking, those stories may be all that remains of lives that slipped too quickly away. Write a *Significant Moments . . .* in the life of a relative of your own.

□ *Now we are on more dangerous ground: my mother's childhood is one thing, my own quite another. This is the moment at which I start rattling the silverware, or ask for another cup of tea* (p. 115). What are the stories most often told about you, and how do you react to them?

Father and Son   *Bernard Mac Laverty*

Bernard Mac Laverty was born in Belfast in 1942. After ten years working as a laboratory technician he went to university in Belfast, and became a teacher. He now lives in Western Scotland. In addition to his two novels, *Lamb* (1980) and *Cal* (1983) (both of which have been successfully filmed), he has to date published three collections of short stories – *Secrets* (Alison & Busby, 1977), *A Time to Dance* (Cape, 1982; Penguin, 1985), from which the present story is taken, and *The Great Profundo* (Cape, 1987). Father-son relationships are explored in both *Lamb* and *Cal*, as well as in a number of the stories. I find Mac Laverty one of the most affecting of contemporary writers.

Ideas for discussion

Father and Son is set in Belfast in the 1970s, in a world in which sectarian killings have become commonplace: in the father's tragic phrase, *The news has come to my door* (p. 124). There have also been personal difficulties: following the death of the mother, the son had disappeared to England, there suffering some kind of addiction from which the father had later rescued him.

Try re-reading the story through the dialogue alone – as if it were a play-script. From the evidence simply of these conversations, what kind of relationship do we have here? The particular form of this story, with its alternating narrators, enables us to enter the minds of both men, and to understand more of what lies behind these exchanges. What things is the Father anxious about? What does the son think of these anxieties? Are these tensions apparent in the *voices* of the narrators?

As a reader of this story, are you clear where your sympathies lie? Are you in any way torn between them? In relation to this question, it is interesting to look again at the pattern of the alternating narrative. We start to read the story from the son's viewpoint. What is our first impression of the father? Where in the narrative do you begin to revise that impression? How important is it that the final page or so of the story is presented wholly through the father's eyes?

Ideas for writing

☐ In *Father and Son* the events are narrated alternately by the characters involved. Try writing your own story in this form, which offers contrasting viewpoints on a single situation.

☐ Write the script for a film of *Father and Son*, using only the available dialogue. The inner thoughts of the two men must then be conveyed through what they do, and how they appear in the film.

☐ In Mac Laverty's novel *Cal* (Penguin, 1984; Heinemann Windmill, 1988) another young man gets caught up in a sectarian killing – though his relationship with his father is very different, and the focus of the story becomes Cal's love for the wife of the man he helped to kill. If you are able to get hold of a copy of the novel, it would be interesting to compare it with the present story.

In the Cutting of a Drink   *Ama Ata Aidoo*

Ama Ata Aidoo was born in 1942 in what was then the Gold Coast, and is now Ghana. She has taught in universities in Ghana, Europe and North America, and has written plays, poetry and fiction. A collection of short stories, *No Sweetness Here*, was first published in 1970, and republished by Longman in 1988. The book deals absorbingly with the complexities of post-colonial Ghana, in which traditional family and village life coexists with the growth of a modern African state.

Ideas for discussion

On first reading, you may have found an initial difficulty in following this story. The opening paragraphs echo the confusion of the speaker, on route from his Fante village to the centre of Accra (the capital of Ghana) and from thence to the city district of Mamprobi. He is visiting one ex-villager, Duayaw, and hoping for news of another, his sister, Mansa, who left home twelve years ago, at the age of ten.

The form of the story, to which most readers will also need to adjust, recreates the situation of oral narration. The only voice we hear is that of the speaker, but in answering the questions of his listeners, and commenting upon their reactions, the speaker creates for us a vivid sense of his audience. By this means, the reader of the story is invited to sit alongside the speaker's uncles, mother and sister, and to share their reactions to the tale.

How would you describe the voice of this speaker? How far is he in control of his story, and of his audience? What is his state of mind? And what does the audience experience as the story develops?

The questions he asks, as much of himself as of his listeners (*Did men buy all these cars with money?*), serve to underline the foreignness to him of city life. What are the things that surprise and disconcert him

179

ʾout the world to which he is introduced by Duayaw? What different values are implied? In the smart world of city bars and dance-halls, the speaker cuts a naive figure. Is he also a comic figure? What do you feel for him? When Mansa laughs at him – *as if the laughter did not come from her stomach* (p. 131), what kind of laughter is it?

What is there to weep about? asks the speaker of his audience at this point. She that was lost is found. Is it a happy ending, therefore? How does he say the repeated words, *Any kind of work is work . . .?*

Ideas for writing

□ In this story, two ways of life are brought into opposition – the life of the traditional Fante villager, and the life of the city to which Mansa and Duayaw have been drawn. How are these worlds contrasted in the story, and where do your sympathies lie?

□ Write Mansa's own story, as told to *her* friends in Accra, in which she describes the encounter with her brother, and what it means to her.

In the Kingdom of the Golden Dust   *Neil Bissoondath*

Neil Bissoondath was born in Trinidad in 1955, emigrating to Canada in 1973. *Digging Up the Mountains* (Andre Deutsch, 1986; Penguin, 1987), from which this story is taken, is his first book: a promisingly rich and varied collection in which Bissoondath's Caribbean origins and the world of black Canadian immigrants are both explored.

Ideas for discussion

When I first read this story, I found it both powerful and haunting, without immediately understanding it. Like much good poetry, it demands an attention to images which the reader must assemble and interpret in his or her own head.

In the Kingdom of the Golden Dust takes place in an unidentified Spanish-American republic during a period of political instability. The town is now in the control of government forces; sometime earlier, however, the townspeople have given refuge to guerilla forces opposed to the state, carrying Russian weapons. Now, the unmarried girls of the town are the unwilling contestants in a competition to choose the Police Queen.

Because of the way the story is written, the reader is not immediately informed of all this, or of the significance of the mysterious opening paragraph. We are drawn into the story through the consciousness of the narrator, seventeen-year-old Maria Luisa – what she observes around her, and the memories and emotions that crowd in on her.

What impression are we given of the town square, and the mood of those assembled there? Where does the sense of tension come from? How does Maria Luisa regard Lisímaco Gonzales?

A glimpse of the green-helmeted Lieutenant Morales on duty in the square leads Maria Luisa to recall vividly *that morning, three months ago* when *the mistake* occurred. How much can we discover about this event? What did it mean to Maria Luisa?

In the second part of the story (p. 136 onwards), the scene in the square recedes in the girl's mind, and in the heat of the sun a sustained hallucination appears to take over. Her memories of the death of Pedro, Miguel and Tomás merge with the separate memory of the young guerilla who had shown her his AK47, and with her own fantasies of revenge.

What emotions are you left with? Is it, in the end, an optimistic story?

Ideas for writing

☐ Which moments in the story convey most sharply the *oppressiveness* of the regime under which Maria Luisa and her friends live? What forms does this oppressiveness take? For Maria Luisa, what kinds of resistance are possible?

☐ Look again at the references in the story to Lisímaco Gonzales, noting his attitude to the crowd, to the girls, to the competition. Then rewrite the scene from Gonzales' viewpoint.

☐ *'You write poetry?' 'Yes.' 'What do you write about?' 'Anything.' 'Flowers? Birds?' 'Yes.' And murder, I want to add* (p. 135) Write the poem that Maria Luisa writes that night.

Learning to Fly   *Christopher Hope*

Christopher Hope was born in Johannesburg, South Africa, in 1944. He now lives and works in England. He has published four novels, some books of poetry, and a volume of short stories entitled *Private Parts* (RKP, 1982; Grafton, 1984), in which the tensions and contradictions of white South Africa are depicted with ferocious

...umour, and from which the present story is taken. The book is banned in South Africa.

Ideas for discussion

Long ago, the story begins, *in the final days of the old regime* . . . The old regime is in fact South Africa as it is at present; the narrator speaks to us from some future time in which the Boer government has been replaced, as in all other African nations, by a majority black regime. This kind of distancing in time or place is a common tactic of 'satirical' writers, whose weapon is ridicule. The device enables them to write about present realities with a pretended detachment. Does anything in the way the story is told – the tone of voice, for example – contribute to this sense of detachment?

The bizarre generalisations of 'du Preez's Law' (p. 142) serve to send up a whole catalogue of prejudices and stereotypes: it is *your average white man* who has *a wonderful sense of rhythm*, whereas *everybody knows* that *your average blackie* believes he can fly. And behind the macabre farce of window-jumping stands the reality of present-day South Africa, in which violent deaths in police custody are commonplace, and blandly improbable explanations routinely offered. How funny is all this?

In Jake Mpahlele, du Preez meets his match: what is most alarming for du Preez is that this man *quite clearly did not hate him* (p. 147). In what ways are the men similar? What do they think of each other? Can you explain why it is Mpahlele, in the end, who proves the stronger?

Compare the final sentence of this story with the opening paragraph. What effect do these echoes have? What are the implications of ending the story in this way?

Ideas for writing

□ *'Yes,'* said Mpahlele, *'we are your children. We owe you everything.'* (p.148) What does Mpahlele mean by this, and in what ways does the story confirm it?

□ Choose some aspect of life in your present society, and use *Learning to Fly* as a model for a story in which you pretend to be writing from some point in the future, looking backwards to the present decade. Try and carry over into your own writing the sense of historical detachment, and the exaggerations that nonetheless point to the truth.

'Do you Love Me?' *Peter Carey*

The Australian writer Peter Carey, born 1943, is the author of four novels, including *Illywhacker* (Faber & Faber, 1985), and *Oscar and Lucinda* (Faber & Faber 1988), and a collection of stories, *The Fat Man in History* (Faber & Faber, 1980), republished as *Exotic Pleasure* (Picador, 1981). Carey is among the most inventive of writers, a deviser of improbable, but nonetheless alarming, fictions.

Ideas for discussion

Like the previous story, this one is set in some future, or perhaps parallel world, which prompts the reader to make connections with the world he or she knows. There are obvious elements of science fiction, and the reader's imagination is kept hard at work. I myself had no difficulty imagining a society with a bureaucratic *passion for lists*, in which material possessions are hoarded, accounted for, and fought over – even a society in which the work of cartographers (map-makers), in recording coastal erosion, is held in the highest esteem. My imagination falters, however, at the notion that parts of a landscape might become *less real* over time, and disappear, though the desire of the government to suppress all knowledge of the fact is again recognisable enough.

What Carey asks us to accept is the idea of *spontaneous dematerialisation*. However improbable the idea may be, the reactions *to* it seem to me to be entirely believable.

As with *Learning to Fly*, the tone is crucial to the writer's purposes. What is the effect of the report form, with its numbered sections? What gives the writing its documentary feel? Look again at section 10, *An Unpleasant Scene*, which I find wholly gripping. Where does the power of the writing in this passage come from?

Alongside the eyewitness accounts of public events, the narrator offers us a more personal memoir of his father during this period. What kind of man is presented here? Is the reader sympathetic? It is the father who interprets what is happening in moral terms: *We no longer love one another. When we realise that we need one another we will stop disappearing* (p. 158). Might that be the moral of the story?

With the father's growing apprehension that he is himself insufficiently loved, that Cartographers as a body are perhaps no longer wanted, the mood of the story changes again. What did you feel as you read the final section? Did you believe what was happening?

Ideas for Writing

☐ By what means does Peter Carey persuade us to believe, for the purposes of the story, in the fact of dematerialisation?

☐ As a leading cartographer, the father is on the inside of what is happening. Write some pages from his private notebook during the period of the story.

☐ Using Carey's tale as inspiration, write a story of your own in which something very odd begins to happen to the world. Try and make the events believable – the report form, as here, might prove a useful device.